MICHAEL PRESLEY'S

BLACKFUNK IV:
CONSEQUENCES

Blackfunk, Inc
Brooklyn,
New York

Cover design:Ty Alston- info@unounmedia.com
Peaches Sterling -Line editing: -harrispat82@hotmail.com
Interior Design: Naval Reid-navalreid@hotmail.com
Special assistance: Allison Braham

Blackfunk, Inc
PO Box 23782
Brooklyn, NY 11202

Publisher's note:
This is a work of fiction. Names, characters, places and incidents either are
the product of the author's imagination or are used fictitiously, and any
resemblance to actual persons, living or dead, business establishments, events
or locales is entirely coincidental.

ISBN-13: 978-0-9705903-4-3
ISBN-10: 0-9705903-4-3

First printing November 2010
Printed in Canada

Dedication

As always to my mom, who continues to be a guiding light
and
My daughter, Meekaya, the angel in my life.

About the Author

Michael Presley made a name for himself in 2001 with his first self-published novel, BLACKFUNK. Not only was Blackfunk a phenomenal success; it spun two other novels: Blackfunk II, No Regrets No Apologies and Blackfunk III, Whatever it Takes. The Blackfunk Trilogy has sold over two hundred thousand copies and continues to be highly requested by readers. In 2007 Michael Presley's fourth novel, Tears On A Sunday Afternoon, was published by Strebor Books, a division of Simon and Schuster. Keisha's Choice a teenage drama was released in March 2009.

Michael Presley has been a guest on numerous radio stations including WLIB and The Wendy Williams show on WBLS. He has also been featured in Black Issues Book Review. His books have been reviewed in Black Women, Heart and Soul and Smooth magazines and also the Caribbean Life newspaper and online at Rawsistaz.com.

Mr. Presley was born in Grenada, to a Grenadian mother and a Barbadian father, then migrated to Brooklyn, New York where he now lives. He attended Wingate High School and went on to Stony Brook University where he received a B.A. in English with a concentration in creative writing. Mr. Presley spent over twenty years working with the Science and Technology Entry Program (STEP) at New York City College of Technology. It is a program that prepares high school students for post secondary education. He combines his passion for writing with his love of martial arts and is presently studying Taoist Tai Chi Kung with Grand Master Roosevelt Gainey.

Mr. Presley has also co-written a screen play for his first novel Blackfunk. He hopes to obtain financing for it and bring it to theatres very soon. He is currently working on two novels, Who is My Father? and Die to Live.

MICHAEL PRESLEY'S

BLACKFUNK IV:
CONSEQUENCES

WWW.BLACKFUNK-BOOK.COM
Xiomara
Web site creator and manager
Xiomara78@gmail.com

WWW.THEBLACKFUNKEXPERIENCE.COM
Ty
Web site creator and manager
info@unounmedia.com

Joel
Web site photographer:
lionoflevi@gmail.com

Chapter 1

I can't do this anymore!" Roger cried out, wiping the tears flowing from his eyes. His hand gripped the wheel tightly as he entered the ramp onto Highway 95. The black Mercedes S500 responded to every movement of his hands. The premium soft gray leather seats, created a bucket that held his massive body.

"What the hell is wrong with you?" Kim asked. She seemed to be getting more and more irritated by Rogers actions. Kim looked stunning in her fitted black and white Versace dress. The seat she held next to Roger was now occupied with her sexy elegance. They were on their way home, after attending a dinner at the exclusive Reba restaurant, located in the heart of D.C. As was expected, Kim had charmed both the men and women at the dinner tonight, held for Senator Pitkin of Washington's third district. Roger behaved like a doting husband, keeping the hungry lions at bay. It was a role he had played exceptionally well this evening, even though he had downed one too many scotch on the rocks. Kim thought that the evening went extremely well, and was looking forward to a peaceful night's sleep. She knew that she and Roger didn't have a perfect relationship, but in this town, who the hell did.

"This is a lie, Kim. We both know it is. I don't understand what happened to us. You're not the sweet girl you were when I first met you. You've changed." Even though the AC was on, Roger was still sweating profusely.

"I don't know what you're talking about, Roger. We had a fabulous dinner, with some of the top politicians in Washington. Who, by the way, unanimously nominated me to become the next Washington Senator! I hope that by you downing the scotch as though it was water, didn't stop you from realizing why we were there. " Kim looked disgustingly at Roger.

"I feel the way you look at me." Roger became infuriated by her arrogance, and he began pounding on the steering wheel, as the car speedometer hit the 95 mark. "No amount of alcohol could stop me from feeling this lump in my throat."

"Grow the fuck up, Roger."

"This relationship is a farce, and a dirty rotten lie!"

A frown appeared on Kim's beautifully painted face. "You had too much to drink tonight," Kim said. "I saw you move from the champagne to the scotch."

"I'm not drunk. It takes more than a few drinks to get me drunk. I'm perfectly fine."

"So, why the fuck are you acting like a bitch?" Kim's frown now turned into anger.

"This is over, Kim. I cannot continue living this way."

"What is over, Roger? Me, working and paying all the bills in the house, while you run around doing useless community events? Your salary barely pays the gas and electric bill. Do you even know how much the mortgage is? Oh, I'm sorry. I forgot you said that finances hurt your head. It hurts your head, because you can't pay for anything."

"It's all about the money with you, isn't it?"

Kim mockingly replied, "No Roger darling, it's all about love."

"Kim, I never thought it was all about love. I've waited five years for you to love me, and it never happened. Five years devoted to you in every possible way. I may be a romantic, but I'm not stupid."

Kim hit the button on the side of the car seat, stretching her long legs, as the seat went back.

"I don't get you, Kim. We did have it all. Don't you think I've made enough sacrifices just to be with you? I had a great job in New York, and then you decided to move to Washington. You didn't even consider my feelings, even though I dropped everything, including my family, so that we could move. Then, when I got here, I couldn't even find a job. Since you already had connections, you were able to secure a good position. Even though our daughter Raqueen was born only a few months after we arrived here, I still did my best to take care of her. You never gave me any credit for that."

"That's what you were supposed to do Roger, she's your daughter."

Roger turned for a second and looked incredulously at Kim. "No, Kim, Raqueen is not my daughter!"

"What are you talking about, Roger? Have you totally lost your mind?"

Kim pressed the button, abruptly bringing the seat up, while straightening her dress.

"Like I said before, I may have been a fool in love, but I'm definitely not stupid. I never told you this, but when Raqueen was two years old, I had a DNA test performed on her, and the results proved what I already knew. As hard as that truth was, I stayed with you and lived the lie. But, I can't do it anymore."

"I don't know what you're talking about," Kim said, refusing to address Roger's statement.

"Kim, please don't go there. Your charm doesn't work for me anymore. You can have all these men and women salivating, but I know the real you. And the real you is the devil reborn. You are not a good person, and this is over."

"No, Roger it's not over. You don't say when it's over, I do. Remember, you're with me- I'm not with you."

"Kim, I understand that the timing might not be right for you, but I can't stay in this relationship anymore. I'm telling you, it's done."

"Let me tell you what's going to happen next. You're going to drive us home, and we'll both have a few more drinks. Then, we'll climb into bed and have mind blowing sex, and afterwards, go to sleep. Tomorrow, you'll take Raqueen to the school like you always do. I'll go to work, and you'll attend your community meeting, just as if nothing happened. And please forget that we ever had this conversation."

"Not this time, Kim. I have another surprise for you. Do you remember that girl Yin that came to our house for Thanksgiving dinner this year?"

"That little Asian girl?"

"She is Chinese, and I've been seeing her for over a year. Tonight, I'm leaving your sorry ass behind and moving in with her. I already took all my clothes from the house, so believe me, this is real."

Kim started to laugh. "Now I get it. This isn't about me and Raqueen. It's because you got stuck in some Asian pussy. You can have the little whore. I don't want you, either."

"Bitch, don't call my woman a whore."

Kim laughed again. "But it's okay you calling your wife a bitch."

"I'm just calling it as I see it."

"You still can't admit to me who Raqueen's father is, even after I raised her all these years as if she were my own, knowing she wasn't."

"Why would I? I've never told you, because you never asked. Do you really want to know? Seeing that we are putting all our cards on the table, I have no problem telling you now."

"You are going to destroy that child. She is such an angel. It's a pity her mother is a fucking bitch. You should have never had her. Some women were not meant to have children, and you're one of them."

"La, la, la, there you go again with your preaching. You starting something that you can't finish. You're so transparent. I knew all along that you were fucking Yin. You are as readable as a first grade book. The funny part is I didn't even care. How did you think I moved up in the firm so quickly? You thought it was all brains? It took a whole lot more than that. You're the one who's pathetic."

Roger sadly shook his head, "How long were you planning to keep up this charade of a marriage?"

"Roger, my boy." Kim took her hand, gingerly playing with his head. "Marriage is a business. Ours was an excellent one. But now you want to put it to an end, because you are "in love." You don't even know what love is."

"Bitch, I could kill you."

"No Roger, that takes balls, and you don't have any. Now let me tell you something about love."

"Kim, I don't want to hear your bullshit anymore."

"Sorry, Roger. You're the one who opened the can of worms, and now it's all coming out."

"Let's just stop this and go our separate ways."

"Roger, don't you get it? I'm not letting you go unless it works out for me! I told you that it's not about you. Raqueen is the product of real love. She is the product of a love I would die for. She is the child of the man that I will grow old with."

"You used me!"

"Roger, you are unraveling. Don't take this so hard. I took the blows you gave *me*."

"I can't believe I loved you for so long. If you love him so much, why aren't you with him instead of me?"

"Everything in due time, Roger, everything in time. But I think you are right about one thing. It is time for me to take Raqueen on a visit to New York. It is time she meets her brother. Raqueen needs to be with him, and I need to be with the only man I've ever loved. This leaves you out Roger, but I still want to give you a proper goodbye. "

"This is too much."

Kim slid her legs over to the driver's side. "No, Roger, it's not. This is our exit."

Kim expertly started unbuttoning Roger's pants.

"Don't do that Kim, its over!" he gasped.

Her head swiftly went down into his lap. When she pulled her wet lips off him, he was moaning and squirming in the seat. She kept her hand on his throbbing dick, while he continued driving. She kept pulling on his dick. She put her foot over Roger's, and onto the accelerator.

"This exit has so many trees on the side of the road, and it's starting to rain. This is not good. I never should have started this. Roger, you look like you're about to…Wait! You don't have your seat belt on! Oh My God! The car is accelerating! I can't believe you're having an orgasm! Roger, stop! We're going to crash!"

The car slammed violently into a tree.

Startled, Kim pushed, and finally pried the car door open, struggling under the weight of the exploded airbags. She looked around, but couldn't find Roger. A huge 80 year old tree was now occupying the space where

Roger had been. Kim grabbed the car door and desperately held on for support, as she tried to get out. There was glass and metal all over the n wet slippery embankment. Through the blinding rain, she blinked her eyes, looking for signs of Roger. Suddenly she found him, sprawled out next to a tree. He was lying in the million dollar reforestation project that the government recently supported. She staggered towards him, with pain and coldness in every step. When she finally reached him, she let gravity pull her down, and fell next to him.

He looked up at her and tried to say something, but the blood flowing from him prevented him from doing so.

"Don't try and speak, Roger. I forgive you. I'm sorry for everything that happened, and I don't want to lose you," She cried, as she gently held his head in her lap.

He tried to respond, but the blood gurgled in his mouth, and he began to choke. Kim tenderly wiped the blood from his mouth, with the hem of her beautiful dress.

"Goodbye, Roger!" She cried, and gently pressed his eyes closed for the last time.

Suddenly, Roger gasped, as his eyes opened wide and looked directly into Kim's eyes. His body then slowly went still.

At that moment, Kim saw the blinking green light in Roger's pocket and pulled out his cell phone. Tearfully, she yelled into the phone, telling the emergency operator about the accident. "Please, hurry! My husband is badly injured!" She hung up and gently lowered his head back down on to the wet grass. She thought about putting her shawl under his head, but knew it was useless. Instead, she threw it around her neck and struggled to stand. The steady traffic heading down 95 North was somehow comforting, and a wave of warmth swept throughout her body. In a strange way, the night wasn't cold and dreary anymore. The realization and longing that she had been away from her real home for five years, was now finally over. She was free. She and Raqueen could now go back to New York. It took the death of her husband to make this possible.

"For the first time in my life, Raqueen will meet her father and her brother," she sighed. "Now, I'm free to marry Rashaun, and we can be the family that we were always meant to be. Sorry Albertina, but your son and I are meant to be together," Kim said to the passing cold wind.

"Rashaun, Rashaun." The voice whispered.

Rashaun lifted his head off the pillow and looked at Andria fast asleep next to him.

"Rashaun, Rashaun." He heard the voice again. He sat up on the bed and looked around him. This time, he saw the little body with his hand around Andria. He smiled, as he bent down and kissed his son. He didn't know when his son had climbed into bed with them.

"Rashaun."

This time, Rashaun recognized his mother's voice. He pinched himself with disbelief.

"Come into the kitchen," his mother instructed.

Rashaun rose from his bed and went into the kitchen. When he entered, he turned on the light below the microwave. He didn't want to wake up Andria.

"Mommy, is it really you?"

"Yes, my son."

"Why are you here? You're supposed to be dead."

"My body is, but not my spirit. My spirit has never left."

"But..."

"Rashaun, don't try to understand."

The kettle whistled and Rashaun drew a tea bag.

"Make one for me, too," she said.

Rashaun looked dumbfounded. "You?"

"No, Rashaun, I won't be able to drink it, but I would like to smell it."

Rashaun took a lemon grass teabag and placed it into the cup. He poured the steaming water over it. He put it down on the table, opposite the chair he had pulled out for himself. Taking the cup, he quietly sat down. He stared at her in apprehension, and lifted the saucer off his cup.

"Mom?"

"I know son, you want to know why I'm here?"

Rashaun slowly nodded his head.

"I never left you, my son. I have always been here. I'm so glad that Madam Unida taught you how to listen."

"Madam Unida taught me how to listen?"

"Yes, Rashaun. If she didn't show you, you never would have heard me. Although I've always been here, I've never spoken to you. I silently watched you become the great husband and father that I knew you were capable of being. I watched, as Wisdom did the same things you used to do as a boy. You have produced a replica of yourself."

Rashaun smiled, "No, Mom, he isn't that bad."

"Yes, he has that same hard head you have."

"Mom, I could never fight with you, so I'm giving up right now."

"That's my smart boy. I see you have been taking good care of your Father."

Rashaun shrugged. "He can be impossible at times, but he is still a good man."

"I know only too well. I lived with him for over thirty years."

"Mom, I don't know if you heard me when I thanked you for all you've done for me. I can't believe I've been given the opportunity to thank you again in person. It seems like you always had the right answers. You always knew what to do, and where to go."

"Not always, Rashaun. I don't always have the answers. There are things I can't always tell you."

"What do you mean?"

"Instead of always looking over you, Rashaun, I now had a need to contact you directly.

"Mom, the last five years have been great. You don't have to worry about me. I have a beautiful wife, and the Lord has blessed me with a great son, Wisdom. My practice has picked up, and everything is great."

"I know, Rashaun. I have been witness to it all."

"What does the future hold for me?" Rashaun asked in a shaky voice.

"Rashaun, do you know what makes a man great?"

"What does that have to do with this conversation?"

"Son, just answer the question."

"It is his ability to do things."

"No, Rashaun. What makes a man great is his ability to listen. You cannot become great if you don't listen."

"I have seen many great men fall," Rashaun answered.

"So have I. Most importantly, do you know their reason for falling?"

"No."

"It's simple. What made them great has been forgotten by them. Now that they have succeeded, they've stop listening. They start believing their own praises, and the people around them. They stop listening to the voice. The voice that made them struggle and persevere, they no longer hear. Instead, they have convinced themselves that they are the ones who are right, and don't need to listen anymore. Madam Unida woke you up with her wisdom. Now, you will follow the right path and become successful. As you go down that path and continue your journey in life, you will stay on the right track. The impossible will now become possible. You will make that happen."

Rashaun pensively held his head in his hand, trying to absorb all the information his Mother shared with him. He became overwhelmed as her voice penetrated his ears, and tears began flowing from his eyes. "How do I…"

"You will know, Rashaun. You will be tested. I cannot predict your future, because I don't know what will happen. I'm here to advise you to just listen to the voice. There are those who will be very skeptical of you when you tell them this. Some will think you're crazy, but don't despair and don't give up. It's the powerful voice that told a man it's time to rule a nation. It's the voice that lives with no regrets and no apologies. You will do whatever it takes to follow. She was determined to make him see the light.

"Will I ever see you again, Mommy?"

"I don't know, Rashaun. It is not always for me to decide. Even my spirit has a guide, and I cannot control everything. I don't know what tomorrow will bring. I came here today, because I needed to tell you to keep listening. You are a great man. Some things in life people thought were impossible, have now become an everyday occurrence. A man doesn't know the future, and therefore you need to make every day count. Life is about action. Every action has its consequences, as well as being idle or doing nothing. Listen to the voice, and live a happy life. That is all I want for you.

"Thank you, Mommy."

"It's time for me to go, my son."

"Mommy, please don't leave!" he pleaded desperately.

"I can't make any promises I'll be back, Rashaun. When it's time, if it's meant to be, you will see me again. Whether we meet as spirits, or body and spirit, I promise, we will see one another again."

"Don't go, Mommy!" he shouted, against the unforgiving howling of the wind outside. Knowing his Mother had abruptly left, Rashaun turned off the light below the microwave and sat back on the chair, feeling bewildered. He stayed there for an hour in the darkness thinking, and then slowly went back into his bedroom. He gently lifted his son up onto the pillows and tenderly kissed his cheek. Grateful for his blessings, he walked over to Andria and kissed her sweet lips, too. This comforted him, and he was able to lie back down on his bed, and finally slept until morning.

Chapter II

"The first time I came into this restaurant, I had to wait to be seated. Now, with the slow economy, we seem to be the only two people here." Rashaun eyes sadly roamed the empty restaurant. "People are really hurting these days."

"Tell me about it. I don't even mind teaching now. Today, health and education seem to be the only jobs not being cut." George followed Rashaun's observation of the makeup of the room. "This is a good thing for me."

"Well, it also means you have to keep spending."

"Not me, Rashaun, I have a child and an ex-wife. That doesn't leave much left for spending," as he rubbed his forehead. "I'm broke now, since my divorce."

Rashaun laughed, "Yeah, I forgot we have switched sides. You enjoy having all those female contacts in your PDA."

"You tell me. I know Andria is great and everything, but don't you miss the game?" George asked.

Rashaun was silent for a few seconds, before replying. "Nah, not really. This year, we'll be celebrating our fifth anniversary. To be honest with you, it feels like this is our first. Andria is a terrific woman, and she doesn't stress me about shit."

"Yeah, I know what you mean. I have moments when I miss my wife, but I made a decision. I know myself. If I was still with her, I would be thinking of the game. Some of us can never be satisfied."

"We want it all, sometimes. Doing the right thing doesn't always work out to be the right thing. There was a time when I thought I would never be able to trust a woman again, but that's in the past now."

"We truly have switched positions Rashaun, because now I don't think *I'll* ever trust a woman again. The game is twisted. Women are grimy users; they would fuck your brother *and* your sister. I've had so many threesomes, it's unbelievable." George just shook his head in amazement.

"I hear you, my brother."

The waitress, oblivious to their conversation, brought their food over.

"You've been through some shit, my brother," George said, as he started to eat his salad. "And now, you're doing good. You got your girl."

"Yeah man, it hasn't been easy. But I'm truly blessed. They say what don't kill you, will make you stronger."

George drank some of his tea. "Things have changed for all of us. I never thought I would substitute a salad for a double whopper."

"For years, I've been telling you to take care of yourself. I told you the shit you ate was no good."

"I guess you telling me is one thing, but when my doctor told me either I change, or go on pills, that kinda woke me up." George continued. "Now, when I see people eating that stuff I used to eat, I want to take it from them, and throw it away."

"Life is a brutal teacher. Some people search for wisdom from others, and some people need it rammed down their throats. Hey, George, don't look now, but this gorgeous woman is coming in."

George swiftly turned around and stared at the woman talking to the waitress.

"I have to go to the bathroom."

"Why the fuck are you telling me that? I don't have to give you permission," Rashaun said, as George jumped out of his seat, and rushed into the bathroom."

"You got the runs?" Rashaun asked so loudly, that the waitress and the woman looked astounded.

Rashaun went back to eating his food. A few seconds later, his phone rang. He picked it up and noticed George's name on the screen. "You all right?"

"I can't come back out," George barked into the phone.

"You that sick?"

"No! That's Rose, the woman I told you about."

"Yeah, you said you been seeing her for a minute."

"I also told her that I had to go to a teacher's conference."

"And?"

"Damn! Man, do I have to spell everything out for you?"

"George ain't no big deal. Just tell her you came back."

"I called her an hour ago and told her that I was still in California."

Rashaun couldn't contain his laughter any longer. "Well let me see, it takes five hours to fly back from Cali, and by my calculations, you have to stay in that bathroom for another four hours. "Uh, oh, George, she just took a book out of her bag. It's a big one, too."

"Rashaun, stop fucking with me."

"George, my food is getting cold. I will call you back."

"Rashaun, don't hang up."

"George, you're getting some company in the bathroom. This guy is about to enter the bathroom, and he's in a serious rush. I hope it's a two stall. Your girl is ordering now. Just sit tight. Maybe she might go to the bathroom or something."

"All right. Call me as soon as she moves."

"Later."

Rashaun continued eating his food. His phone vibrated, and it was George again.

"Rashaun, this guy's got diarrhea, and you can't believe the sounds that are coming from the bathroom. Oh my God, and the smell! I never knew shit could smell so bad."

"Hang in there my brother, but please don't call me to talk about shit while I'm eating."

"Damn, Rashaun, this shit ain't funny."

"There you go, talking about shit again."

"I'm going to pass out."

"George, I think she's going to be here for a while. Now, she's taking out her cell phone to call someone."

"Damn, she's calling me."

"Go handle your business playa, and maybe you can get her to leave the restaurant."

"What the fuck I'm going to tell her?"

"Think of something!"

Rashaun looked over at the woman, and suddenly her facial expression changed, but she continued her conversation on the phone. She was constantly moving her chair now, and kept looking down at the floor. In the space of five minutes, she had picked up her bag, and was hurrying out the door. Rashaun's phone rang again.

"What the fuck did you tell her?"

"I told her that the restaurant was on the news, an inspection was done and they found the largest mice infestation in Brooklyn. I'm coming out now."

"How you know she would leave?"

"She had called me over to her place one night, because there were dead mice on her kitchen floor. When I got there, she had locked herself in her room. I had to get the Super to get into her apartment. She spent two weeks at her mother's place, and then moved out of the apartment."

"You are a bad man."

Rashaun hung up the phone.

George came out, adjusting his clothes as he walked.

"How many damn restaurants do they have in Brooklyn? Out of all of them, she chose this one to go to this evening.."

"Look at the bright side. At least she wasn't here with another man."

George raised his eyebrow and said, "And you think I give a damn? You and I know, people will do what people want to do. I ain't gonna stop that."

"Are you going to finish eating?"

George shook his head. "After what that guy put down in the bathroom, there's no way I'm eating for the rest of the night."

Rashaun looked at his phone. "I told Andria that I'd be home by six."

George laughed and said, "She's got you on the ball and chain, man."

"Nah, never that. I just like to be a man of my word. I haven't been home at a decent hour all week. I'm sure she's cooking something, and I promised to help pitch in."

"You really like that married life, don't you?"

"Yeah, I do. Like I said, Andria doesn't stress me. She makes me want to come home."

"Yeah, well I'm going to holla at this chick. Maybe I'll go by her house tonight."

Rashaun paid the bill, and left the restaurant with George.

Rashaun turned the key in the lock, trying his best not to make a sound.

"Forget it, he's not home. Your father came and got him earlier, and said he will keep him tonight," Andria shouted from the kitchen.

"You heard me!"

"Rashaun, a deaf man could have heard you."

"Stop it! I wasn't that loud."

"Okay Baby, whatever you say."

Rashaun put his briefcase down and walked into the kitchen.

Andria was at the counter, cutting up some carrots.

"I see you have my shirt on again. I need that shirt right now." Rashaun said as he walked up behind Andria. He put his arms around her. "Can I have my shirt, Baby?"

"Since I washed it, I get to keep it."

"Then, I will have to give you the pants I'm wearing right now, too."

"Yep, I want that, too."

Rashaun started to kiss Andria at the back of her neck.

Andria started to tremble, "Rashaun, I won't be able to finish cooking if you don't stop."

Rashaun continued to kiss Andria, as he reached over and unbuttoned the two buttons of her shirt. He slipped the shirt off Andria's shoulders, and it fell to the floor. Andria was now completely naked. "I see you were prepared."

She turned around and reached up and held Rashaun's face in her hands. "I'm always prepared for you."

"I so love you," Rashaun said, as he brought his lips to Andria's tender mouth.

"Not as much as I do, you," Andria replied, passionately kissing Rashaun's neck, while her hands reached to unbutton his shirt.

He helped her with the buttons, as their mouths interlocked. He ran his fingers gently down her smooth back. His lips moved from her mouth, to her nose, her eyes, cheeks, and chin. He showered her face with soft, passionate kisses. He reached his hand over to cup her perfectly rounded ass.

She kissed his chest, pulling softly on his nipples as she went down to his naval. Her mouth sucked gently, as her wet tongue darted in and out of his mouth. She worked her mouth all the way down to his ankle, and slowly licked her way up to the inside of his thighs, teasing him as she went along. His erect penis stood above her head, tantalizing her, as she grasped him with her hands, and began kissing his scrotum. Slowly, her tongue worked its' way up and down the shaft of his penis. He threw his head back and gasped for air, as she slowly put his head into her mouth. She then worked her mouth up and down his penis, enjoying the taste and feel of him in her mouth. He grasped her head and held her tightly, as his penis went in and out of her mouth. He controlled her head with his hands, sending her back and forth. At this point, it took all his willpower to keep from having an orgasm. He wanted to make it last. Slowly, he pulled her mouth away from him. As she rose up, he went down.

Wanting to devour her, his kisses became hungry and forceful. He reached down and parted her legs with his hand. His hand slid under her legs, as she looped her arms around his neck. He lifted her off the floor and she sat on him, urgently wrapping her legs around his biceps. He pulled her to him, slipping his tongue deeply into her wet crevices. She groaned loudly, as his tongue continuously worked from the outside in. In the heat of passion, she pulled his head into her, his tongue now resting squarely on her clitoris. She worked his bald head vigorously back and forth, almost suffocating him, as her body started to convulse into an orgasm. A stream of warm fluid sprayed from her vagina onto his face. Gently, he took her down from his shoulders and placed her onto the ground. She rested her trembling hands on the chair, and arched her back to receive him. He drove into her, gently and slowly at first, feeling each muscle in her warm vagina clamp down on his penis. His strokes were long and smooth, penetrating deeply inside of her. She eagerly met every one of his thrusts, pushing back into him, as his penis engulfed the far reaches of her vagina. He was so far into her, that he was touching places only he could do. He alternated his strokes from long to short, feeling her excitement building and heard her moaning. He knew this was the only place to be. He totally felt her, that unique feeling he was waiting for, when their bodies melted into one. The movements of her body urgently changed now, and so did his. His thrusts became harder and even deeper. Her sounds were unrecognizable, as she got closer to climaxing. It was their code of passion, and they were good at it.

She felt him, too. He knew her body well, the same way she knew his. They roughly bucked against each other now, like two wild animals. Their passion was ferocious, tagging every ounce of energy from one another. Their body movements were now unrecognizable. It was the pure dance of pleasure. Her head gave way to the passion, as her body started to shake. He groaned, as she felt him send his army of love deep inside her. She continued to shake like a crazy bull, unable to control her passion. He held onto her tightly, and then slowly released her, as her body finally weakened. They both slumped down onto the ceramic kitchen floor. He pulled her to him, and cradled her in his arms.

"Now look what you've done," she said, making herself comfortable in his arms.

"Why do I always get blame?" He asked.

"Because you know that spot, and you always go for it."

"You know what, I'm going back out. I can't take this."

"No you not. Seeing that I'm finished cooking. We are going to eat, and then go another round or two."

"Wisdom is getting a sister tonight."

"I'm game. And you promise you're not going to fall asleep on me?"

Andria slowly got up. "Do I look like I'm about to go to sleep?"

"I will give you 45 minutes after dinner."

"Not even an hour."

Rashaun went over to Andria, who was now cutting up green peppers. He took her hand.

"Baby, I got the rest of this. Sit down and I'll finish up."

"Are you sure?

Rashaun guided her to the chair. "I got this."

"You shouldn't have made me come. You know how you wear me out."

Rashaun took a head of lettuce from the fridge. He washed it, and began to cut it up. He went back into the refrigerator, and got some fresh spinach. He then cut up some tomatoes.

"Andria."

Rashaun turned around to look at Andria. She was fast asleep on the chair.

"My girl didn't even make it twenty minutes."

He put the food back into the refrigerator. He lifted her up, and carried her into the bedroom.

"You ready?" Andria mumbled.

"It's okay, Baby. Go back to sleep." He kissed her, as she hugged the pillow. He sat down next to her and watched her sleep.

"I'm truly blessed."

It wasn't that there weren't many beautiful women in Washington, D.C. There were a lot of them. On any given night, you could find them in many exquisite restaurants in the city, sometimes by themselves, or with others. Their company didn't attract as much attention as the women themselves did. Some of these women liked both men and women, because that's how it is today. This is 2010, and women freely look at other women with devouring eyes, just as men do. It's not a secret anymore. That's just life. Rochele was sitting at the table, sipping fine red wine. The kind that costs $200 a bottle. She was able to afford such an expensive bottle of wine, because she was married to multimillionaire, Cavaka, one of the richest men in D.C.

Rochelle is a beautiful black woman, and she knows it. When she first walked into the restaurant, most of the patrons gave her an "Oh, she is pretty," look, whether spoken verbally or not. She was a real head turner. Glancing down at her gold watch, she reached for her phone, when suddenly the restaurant door opened. Her friend Kim strolled in, and she knew without looking, it was her, by all the "god damn, she's beautiful" comments swirling around her. Kim always got that kind of attention. She laughed inwardly, remembering a time when she visited Kim at criminal court. Kim had just prosecuted a man for murder, and was about to await sentencing. The judge asked the defendant if he had anything to say. He replied, "If I could have one night with Kim Rivers, I'd go merrily to the death chamber." That's the type of impact her beauty had on everyone.

"Girl, if I had what you got, I don't know what I would do with myself," Rochelle said, as Kim kissed her on the cheek. She sat down on the opposite side of the table.

"Did you order yet? I know I'm a little late, but I had to sign some important insurance papers," Kim said, looking exhausted.

"How much you getting?"

"Two mil each for Raqueen and I."

"Wow, that man really loved you and his daughter." Rachelle said.

"Yeah, at one time he did."

"You're now set up for a long time, even though I know you already have a lot of money."

"Yeah, my parents recently put me in charge of their estate. I didn't realize it is worth over 100 million," Kim said, looking at the menu.

"Girl, you got everything going for you."

"Not everything."

"Well, I know you lost Roger, but I'm sure you have men breaking down your door."

"I'm going to New York for a month, and when I come back, I'll have everything."

Suddenly, Rochele looked very irritated, "Kim, don't start that again."

"What are you talking about?"

"I'm talking about your obsession with that lawyer from Brooklyn. Two years ago, I had to talk you into staying with Roger.

"Remember, you wanted to leave your family and go back to Brooklyn to be with that man?" The waiter came over and stood patiently, waiting to take the ladies orders.

After he left, Kim looked over at her friend. "Without him, I could have Oprah money and Obama power and still be unhappy. Rochele, I need him the way I need air to breathe. The more I stay away from him, the more I feel like I'm suffocating."

"Are you listening to yourself, girl? You're talking like the brother got oxygen dick or something, like you need him to live. I've had big dicks, and small dicks, and after a while, they're all the same. I know you like dark shiny black men, so we can go to Africa and bring one back. Whenever you want, we can make that trip."

Kim was now totally annoyed and glared at her friend. "You just don't fucking get it. You think any man could replace him? I tried that. I tried to replace him with others for eight years. It didn't work. I've made up my mind, either I will live with him, or die without him."

"Are you listening to yourself? You think you're the only one? Let me tell you something about myself. Do you think Cavaka was ever my true love?"

The waiter came and delivered the food. He attempted to say something, but the look on the ladies faces made him disappear without opening his mouth.

"My true love is a broke ass big belly man, living in Atlanta with five kids, a wife and numerous girlfriends. At the age of twenty, he was a star athlete on our college basketball team. We were going at it crazy every night. I never had so much fun with someone in my entire life. But, I'm certainly not going back to recreate the past. Hell, no. The past is a memory that doesn't exist in the present, or the future. Cavaka is my husband now, and we have two beautiful kids and live a happy life in Washington, D.C."

Kim placed her fork down and patted her mouth with a white cloth napkin.

"You call what you have with Cavaka happiness? Rochele, it seems you forgot who you're talking to. You forgot how we met. We met, because you wanted to eat my pussy, and your husband wanted to fuck me in the ass. You came waltzing over to me, dripping in diamonds and your fancy designer dress, to see if I was hungry enough. You tried tempting me to go away to the Caribbean with you and your husband."

"I can't believe you brought that up after all these years."

"I brought it up, because I'm tired of listening to your bullshit. You are never happy unless you have a clit between your lips. You, with all that bullshit about living the great life on the hills, doesn't fly with me. If God comes today, Washington will be the first place he burns down, because it is such a city of superficial make believe."

"Oh, and your precious New York will be saved? The city of sin and corruption!"

"The difference between D.C. and New York, is that we know and accept it for what it is. I have never met such fake people before in my life. The whole town is pretentious, including our new President."

"I don't care about all that, because Cavaka and I have been married for over 15 years."

"And that's supposed to mean something? Just look at where we are. We're in Washington, a city based on lies. There are men here that have been married for forty years, and have never even touched their wives. We all know, it is what it is. But to think that this is Utopia, is fucking crazy."

"I can't tell you what to do with your life. You are a big girl now. But I'm warning you, the road you're heading down will only lead to sadness."

"Ro, let me put it this way. I think I have one last time to make it right with my soul mate. If I don't do this now, I will always keep wondering, what if. While I understand your life, and I'm sure you have convinced yourself that you're happy, I can still believe in my own dreams. The day I stop dreaming, will be the day I stop breathing. I have accepted that. I came here to tell you that I'm leaving for New York on Friday and hopefully, I will be gone for no more than a month."

"Are you taking Raqueen?"

"Definitely, of course. Raqueen is the glue that will make us bind, whether he wants us to, or not."

"What are you talking about?"

"I think our food is getting cold. Let's eat first."

After their animated conversation, the ladies ate mostly in silence, only occasionally commenting on the state of politics, and friends they really didn't care about. They left the restaurant at seven p.m. Rochele motioned for her driver, and Kim jumped into her Land Rover Discovery. Kim had picked it up at the dealership earlier this week. The car dealer, a short pudgy white man, didn't even blink an eye, when she said that she was paying in cash. He then informed her that he would have to report the sale to the IRS. He wanted to know if she had any problem with that, otherwise he was willing to work around it. For a fee, of course. Kim declined his offer. After all, she had nothing to hide from the United States government. Roger's will supplied her with more money than she actually needed. Any man she dated, would now jump at a chance to marry her. She had everything going for her; with looks to kill, a career headed for greatness, and a huge bank account. The American dream had come true everything but the man she wanted. While that made him priceless, it made her even more determined to get him back. She was ready to use everything in her arsenal to get him. This was do or die.

Chapter III

*T*he sand felt warm beneath his feet, as Banjo Roberts walked along the beach. Banjo was his birth name but everyone called him Fish and that's the name he went with. The cool Caribbean breeze languished in the air, making it appear cooler than the hot eighty five degrees. He was a tall, slim man with modest muscles, formed by countless hours swimming in the blue waters of his homeland, Montego Bay, Jamaica. The dark color of his skin was not only a testament to his parent's genes, but also produced by the permanent tan he received from working in the sun on his small fishing boat.

Fish waved to the woman, who was cooking with a coal pot by the sea. He was certain that she was making fish tea from the fish he had given her earlier. The haul from the nets was good this morning, after the stormy weather had passed through his country. He had sold enough fish for this month's rent, just from that one haul. His wife, Mindi, would be happy to see him bring some money home for a change, although she was still angry with him. Even though Banjo had spent the entire morning in the water, he could never get enough of the sea. It called to him, like a hooker putting on a fishnet stocking, in an open window.

He pulled his white vest over his head and placed it on a stone, under an almond tree. He walked slowly towards the edge of the water and lifted his legs up faster, as he started to run. His powerful legs propelled him forward against the force of the ever deepening water. Then, as if being shot from a cannon, his whole body catapulted up from the water, and stayed in the air for a few seconds, before breaking the plane of the water again, with his head first. As he dived into the water a second time, his hands became a wide propeller, pushing him through the water, like an Olympic diver. When his head finally burst above the surface, he had traveled many yards out into the blue. His nickname, "Fish," had more to do with his swimming abilities, rather than his looks. He pushed his feet effortlessly to stay afloat in the water, as the noise of an Air Jamaica airplane continued it's decent into the airport. In a week, he would be on one of those big birds, traveling to the United States.

Once more, he elevated himself into the water, and started to swim further out into the ocean. As he swam, he felt the presence of his younger brother behind him, trying to catch up to him. They both learned to swim as children with their father. Fish knew even then, that swimming was his passion, and he became addicted to the blue waters. They would race out to the buoy and back again. Sometimes, Fish would let his brother win, and other times, he would leave him alone out in the blue. When his little brother finally pulled up to the shore, Banjo would have a snow cone waiting for him. Fish missed his brother deeply. At the tender age of twelve, he left Jamaica with their mother, to make a better life in the land of opportunities, a place called "America". But he missed him more than ever now, because he wasn't even in America anymore. Paul Roberts, Banjo's youngest and only brother, was tragically shot twelve times, by Rashaun Jones, a lawyer residing in Brooklyn, New York. Fish would never see him again.

Fish started swimming slowly back towards the shore line. His pent up anger and need for revenge, fed the muscles in his body. His brother's death would not go unpunished, it was a promise he had made to himself. No one, not even his beautiful wife Mindi, could stop him. Fish walked towards the almond tree, and picked his vest up off the stone. He threw it over his right shoulder, and continued to stroll back to his boat. Although he had already taken out the engine and washed it down, he remembered he still had a few lobsters left in it, and wanted to take them back to the hotel on his way home. He didn't get very far, when he heard Ms. Jennifer calling to him.

"Fish, I got some tea for you," Jennifer said, walking towards Fish with a bowl that had a white cloth underneath. "It's hot, so you can't drink it fast."

Fish knew better than to turn down the fish tea from Ms. Jennifer. Although he knew his wife had a big plate of food waiting for him at home, he couldn't refuse. Ms. Jennifer's daughter and her grandkids migrated to the U.S. over ten years ago. They would come back to visit every summer, but Banjo hadn't seen them yet this year. He accepted the bowl graciously from Ms. Jennifer, and turned to walk away.

"I heard you're going to America," she said, as she turned to walk back to the patio.

Fish didn't know exactly what time it was, but he knew it was getting late and he had to get on his way back home. She was being so kind, and he couldn't just walk away. So, he followed Ms. Jennifer to the patio and sat on the chair, that she motioned to him. "Yeah, I have to go there and take care of some family business," he said. Even though Fish hadn't told Ms. Jennifer that he was going to the States, he knew it was a waste of time trying to find out who did tell her. Once something was uttered in this community, everyone knew about it.

"My daughter is always asking me to go there, but America is for young people. America ain't got nothing for me."

"Well, I'm not going to stay long. I just have to take care of some personal business."

"Your brother Paul died over there, didn't he?"

"Yeah, a few years ago."

"Did you go to the funeral?"

"No, I couldn't get a visa at the time. I just got one the other day."

"I remember Paul. He was a good boy when you and him weren't stealing my mangoes."

Fish smiled, mischievously. "You didn't mind?"

"I minded when you all broke my window, pelting stones at the mango. You all could run, boy."

Fish remembered that incident vividly. The mango that they were trying to get wouldn't fall, no matter how hard they shook the tree. As a last attempt, they started throwing stones at it. They managed to hit it a few times, but not enough to make it fall. Being the big brother, Banjo mustered all his strength, and threw the stone with all his might. He managed to hit the mango, but the stone went right through Ms. Jennifer's window and shattered it. They left the mango, and ran all the way home, thinking that the police were after them in hot pursuit.

"Yeah, I'm truly sorry about that."

"That was a long time ago. The mango tree got uprooted in the big storm."

After that incident, he and his brother, Paul, never passed too closely to the house again.

"I'm going to miss you, Fish. You are the only one that always brought me fish."

"Don't worry, Ms. Jennifer, Lantern is going to take care of you and bring you fish while I'm gone."

"I'm going to like that. Fresh fish is good for the old bones. I could never get there in time to get any when the boats come in, since this right foot's been bothering me." Jennifer stretched out her right foot and began rubbing it. She continued, "A lot of people go to America and don't come back, you know."

Fish looked out at the setting sun. "Yeah, I know."

"Never been to the U.S., and don't want to go to that place. Jamaica is sweet enough for me. I was born here, and I'm going to die here." Ms. Jennifer slowly rose from her chair, "You finish with that?"

"Yeah, thank you. You sure make the best fish tea." Fish also rose from his chair.

"Come by before you leave. I got something for you to bring to my daughter."

"Will do," Fish replied, and he walked down her steps.

He went back to his boat and finished cleaning it, taking a quick bath with the same hose he used to clean the boat. The water cascaded down from his short dreads, onto his skin. He shook his head a few times to get the sand out of it. He didn't want to, but knew he would have to go by to see his cousin, Desiree, so that she could get the remainder of the sand out of his hair. He knew he'd wind up sitting with her for at least two hours, and have to listen to her complain about how bad Jamaican men were. Even though she had three children from the bad Jamaican men, it made no difference. He dried his skin off, and walked five minutes to his car, parked up on the hill. He carried a plastic bag filled with an eight foot crab and the lobsters. A tourist from the States had asked to buy the crab from him, but he turned down the offer. His wife loved those crabs, and he was saving it for her. He knew she would be all over him when he walked in with his catch. She might even forget for a minute that he was traveling to the U.S. in a week.

As he drove away from the water and through the country, he

admired the beauty of his homeland, with its greenery and peaks and valleys. The roads were rough, but they became smoother as he drove closer to town. On every corner, there stood a group of grazing goats. Ackee and mango trees adorned almost every front yard. He drove up to a small boarded house that his uncle helped build. The house had two bedrooms, a bathroom, kitchen, and living room that occupied one space. It was now seven o'clock, and his wife Mindy must have just finished cooking. He walked in from the back door, smelling strong stewed chicken. The back door of the house led directly into the kitchen. Sure enough, there stood Mindy, cooking over the small four burner stove.

"Fish, I see you finally got here," she said, not even turning around to look at him.

"Smells good," he said, kissing her on the cheek.

"If it smells so good, how come you leaving me to go to America?"

Fish just shook his head. He really wasn't in the mood to deal with this. "Baby, I got to go to the U.S."

"Sharon from my job said that her husband went to the States five years ago. He said once he gets there, he would send for her and the kids. She's still waiting for him, along with her five kids. He doesn't send her any money and never calls the kids. It's like they don't exist anymore. I don't want that happening to me, too."

"Min, I'm not like that."

"They say those American women are man hungry. I see how they act when they come into the store. They just be wanting to rape those men, and you know damn well that Jamaican men are quick to jump on them."

"Girl, would you stop that. I ain't leaving you for no American woman. You forget they come to the wharf, too. You don't see me running away with them. I come home to you every night."

"Fish, I don't want to lose you. I don't have all the things the American women have, but everything I have belongs to you. I really don't want to lose you." Tears began to fall from Mindi's eyes, while she gripped a big spoon tightly in her right hand.

Fish came up behind her and took the spoon away. He turned the stove off, and gently brought her over to sit down on the chair in the kitchen. As he held her in his arms, his fingers ran over the white spots on her hand. It was the result of a fire that occurred when she was only eighteen years old, and it took the life of her parents, her brother, and her sister. Mindy was the sole survivor of the family now, and her family home had now turned into ashes. Mindi stood five feet five, and was a beauty queen by anyone's standard. Her ample breasts stood erect against her flat stomach, and she had one of those onion butts that men always go crazy for. Her legs were long and strong, and her walk was as seductive as a temptress. It was that walk that had Fish hooked from the start, causing him to knock stuff off in the supermarket, as he shouted to her, "What up, gal?" She didn't answer him at first, but he was very persistent. Eventually she gave in, and that very day, he took her home with him. They had been together ever since.

"Min, I told you, me nah gonna stay in the U.S. Girl, my life is in Jamaica. You are in Jamaica. Me, Fish, I can't stay away from the water. Down by the water is weh me born, and that's weh mi a go die. Seriously."

Mindi looked him right in the eyes. "I don't care what you do in the States. Me being honest. I want you promise me one thing."

"Wha dat?"

"You will come back."

"Mi, ah just told you, mi nah gonna stay in the U.S. I'm going over there and take care of me brother business, and ah coming home. I promise that, if that's wha you want."

"Fish, ah me kill you if you lie for me."

"Me no lie, I swear, me ah come back. I'm leaving everything here with you. If me did wanted to go to America, me woulda gone a long time ago. Now, open the bag and see what me ah bring for you."

Mindi went over to the bag and twisted it open. "You got one!"

"Me, ah told you I was going to."

"We eating it tomorrow. We'll go to the market, and we'll get some things to cook with it. Now, go bathe the boy. I got something for you after dinner."

"Me got something for you too, and it's big and black."

Fish went into the small black and white bedroom that contained a twin size bed. Mindi had packed most of his clothes in a black suitcase. He walked over to the closet and reached up to a shelf at the top. He felt around until he found the leather case, and brought it down. It was approximately eight inches long, and about three inches wide. He reached into it, and pulled out a knife that had a faded wooden handle. He brushed the razor sharp knife against the palm of his hand. His palm became red, as blood flowed to the face, and remained under his skin. Fish and Paul had cut a lot of coconuts with this knife, and it was still very sharp. They always competed to see who could climb up the coconut tree the fastest. Then, they would gather all the coconuts under the tree, and take turns opening them. Once they finished drinking the water, they looked for a stone, and hit the coconuts until they opened up, and scooped out the jelly. He put the knife back into the worn leather case, and walked over to the suitcase that leaned heavily against a small table. He had one more thing he needed to do with the knife. As he stashed the knife between his clothes, memories of his and Paul's life in Jamaica, flashed through his mind. Yes, he knew he was doing the right thing. There was no justice done, when his brother was shot numerous times in the chest. Now, vengeance would be served, with the knife that lay between his shirt and pants, inside of the black suitcase. Once justice was completed in America, Fish would then be able to return to his country and live with his woman, and be near the water that he loved so much.

Chapter IV

*M*ost people don't understand love. Love is a curse, as well as a blessing. People laugh at others, when they see them make fools of themselves, all in the name of love. Love has killed more people in the world, than any disease known to man. It has also healed more people, than any medicine ever could. Kim knew how powerful love was, and understood it all too well. She had prosecuted so many people that killed, hurt, and stole, all in the name of love. Love can be a fucking trap, and she walked right into it. She hated herself for that weakness, as her eyes remained transfixed on the office entrance. Was she a victim, or only a contestant for love? Will she fall, like so many before her, a victim of the illusion of love? She looked around at people busily running their errands. Could they peer into her truck and understand what she was going through? Had they given up on love, or were they overpowered by it, or gravitated towards it, like grass towards a lawn mower? She walked away from a town where men and women would kiss her ass, and anyone else's in the city. She was about to become the epitome of success in Washington, a true politician. But she knew that this position would never give her real happiness. Not if she didn't have the man that God made especially for her. Kim knew that happiness was worth living for, as well as dying for.

The Land Rover, her accomplice, was parked a block away from 5710 Bergen Street. The address was where the office of Jones, Rashaun, Criminal Attorney at Law, was located. Kim sat in the passenger seat at a perfect vantage point, enabling her to see the people entering and exiting the office. She had the New York Times to read, while she waited for Rashaun. She felt a little nervous after not seeing him for nearly two years. The last time she saw him, he was in court, defending a woman accused of child neglect. At the time, she was able to watch him from outside the courtroom, through a glass panel in the door.

Today, she was dressed in a pale blue sweat suit with the word, "Blackfunk" inscribed on the rear of the pants. It was a comfortable outfit that she wore on numerous occasions, when she jogged around the monument in Washington. When she had pulled up there at 7:00 a.m., she took the parking spot of a blond woman, who had scurried into her car, carrying a briefcase. Then she quickly drove off. She smiled, remembering the many times she had been just like that woman. Suddenly, she saw the green ML 320 pull up in front of the office.

Rashaun waved goodbye to the occupants in the car, who were most likely his wife and child. She anxiously waited for him to open the office door and go upstairs. His office was located on the second floor of the building. She knew that his secretary would be arriving at work at 9:00 a.m., so she needed to get there earlier. She got out of the car and started to walk towards the office.

"Damn, sister you are fine!" A man jogging by said, as he went past Kim. Kim ignored the car that stopped, and waited for her to cross the street. She smiled at the young man who nearly fell off his bike, while looking at her. A street vendor offered her a free copy of the latest book written by Nancey Flowers, and all she had to do was give him her phone number. The man behind the counter stopped pouring the coffee for the woman he was serving. She was wearing a gray business suit, and just a few minutes ago, was in a rush to leave. Now, she had all the time in the world.

"I would do her from head to toe," the man behind the counter said.

"Me, too." The woman wearing the business suit agreed, even though she wore a wedding ring on her finger.

Kim rang the doorbell and was buzzed in the door leading to the office. The door was left slightly open, and it creaked as she extended it out.

"Thanks for coming early Tony, there is a slight leak coming from the window," Rashaun said, walking out of his office, wearing a white shirt and multicolored tie.

"Hello, Rashaun." Kim said.

Rashaun didn't speak at first, because he was so shocked, that he didn't know what to say. This was like history repeating itself, the kind that people wished had never happened in the first place. It was like the killing of John F. Kennedy, or the assassination of Martin Luther King. They were events that happened, but no one wanted a re-occurrence of them. As was expected, his shock now turned to anger.

"Kim, what the fuck are you doing here?"

Ignoring his question, she asked, "How are Andria and Wisdom?"

"Kim, I don't have time for this bullshit."

"Rashaun, for someone you have so much history with, you sure are being rude. I came all the way from Washington to visit you, and this is the welcome I get?"

Rashaun thought about his mother. She had come to him for a reason, and that reason was standing right in front of him now. He thought he had dealt with that problem, but thinking and doing, do not necessarily follow one another. He knew that Kim was there for some reason, and knowing her, he doubted that it was for a good one. Somehow, he knew he had to deal with it. He inhaled deeply, and stepped aside, motioning Kim into his office. "Let's deal with this now."

"Thank you," Kim said, and walked into Rashaun's office, working the subtle moves in her hips, that would turn a gay man straight.

◎◎◎

"Thank you, Andria," Robin said, as they stepped out of the elevator.

"Ten years of marriage, that's a long time," Andria said, as she walked along the waterfront with Robin.

"Yeah, lately I have been feeling every day of it." Robin looked out into the clear waters of the Hudson River.

"That doesn't sound too good." Andria remarked, and she looked over at her friend, who was now preoccupied with an NYPD patrol boat that was in the water.

"Do you think they catch any terrorists in these waters?"

Andria looked a little puzzled. "I guess they will, if someone tries to blow up the city with a boat. Robin, what's going on?"

"They're just doing their job."

"I guess you can call it that."

"That's how I feel lately, after being married for ten years. I'm just doing my job."

"I didn't know."

"What is there to know?"

"Robin!"

"Going to this restaurant was great. I always passed by it, but never have been up there. I was so excited to go and eat there. The ride in the elevator, along with the lights of New York City was great. Once we arrived, we found the service and the food to be excellent. Then, during the ride down, and each step of the way, I got the feeling that it was over."

"Robin, are you guys getting a divorce?"

"No, nothing like that. It's just that lately I have been feeling like our relationship is going downhill. It seems like we had been to the top, and now there is no other place to go, but down."

"I'm sorry."

"There is nothing to be sorry about it's just the way life is."

A dark cloud swept over Andria. It was as if her future had just been shattered. She had always looked upon Robin's marriage as ideal. Now, her friend was talking as if her marriage was about to end.

Robin saw the sad look in Andria's eyes. "Andria, my marriage is not over, we are only going through a tough period, that's all."

" Robin, you and Greg have been so good together. It seems like there is never any drama in your lives."

"There is drama, but not the kind that you and Rashaun experience."

"What do you mean?"

"Come on Andria, your relationship with Rashaun is like giving a crack head meth. He was going crazy before, but with the meth, he is now completely gone."

Andria started to laugh, "I guess you right, girl. I have been happy the last two years, and there has been no drama."

"Yeah, you and Rashaun always seem to be on a high when you all are together." Robin stopped and her eyes swelled up. "Greg and I used to be like that."

"I know, and I'm sure you guys will be like that again."

Andria put her arms around her best friend. "Let's go have some ice cream!"

"Girl, do you see the weight I have put on?"

"Look at me! I ain't skinny no more. Rashaun is always telling me that if I put on another pound, he is going to enter me in the biggest loser contest."

"He still goes to the gym regularly?"

"Yeah, I don't think he will ever stop going to the gym. I told him that I will start going with him on Monday."

"Are you?"

"I told him that two months ago."

"Butter Pecan sounds good."

"Wisdom looks just like you." Kim placed the family portrait back down on Rashaun's desk. "How old is he now? Five or six?"

"Five."

Kim put a picture of Raqueen in front of Rashaun. "She will be five, soon."

Rashaun kept looking at the picture of the little girl. She looked very much like Wisdom. He kept staring at the picture, until Kim picked it back up and put it in her purse.

"Kim. I have a long day today, so can we get to it?"

"Get to what Rashaun? I can't come by to see a good friend?"

"Kim, we stopped being friends years ago. Now, either you tell me what you want or you'll have to leave."

"My husband died. Did you know that?"

"No, I'm sorry for your loss."

"Yeah, well tomorrow is not promised to anyone. I just came by to tell you that I was back in town, and thought that maybe we can go out to dinner sometime. With your wife, of course." Kim started to walk toward the door.

"Thanks for the offer, but I would rather not."

"Don't be like that, Rashaun. I know I have done some things in the past, but sometimes we have to move on. Who knows, maybe we can be friends one day."

"I doubt that, Kim. Sometimes things happen for the best. You and I not being together is the best thing that ever happened to me. Like you said, sometimes we have to move on. I did, and I hope you will, too."

"Well, you know me, I got to go work out. You look like you still go to the gym. Maybe we can work out together. I have gotten much stronger."

"Goodbye, Kim."

Kim climbed into her truck, and immediately a car pulled up behind her, waiting for her to move to get the parking spot. Downtown Brooklyn, New York, always a hustle. She sat back in the truck, ignoring the car that was waiting. She had to regain composure of herself. Rashaun had her shaken up. This is the effect she had on men, not the other way around. Finally, she pulled out of the parking space and turned down towards the Flatbush Avenue extension.

Rashaun seemed to be in a good place with his life. She either had to show him that there is a better place being with her, or make his good place a living hell. She turned onto the ramp that would take her from the BQE, to the Belt Parkway. She was going to have to enter his world to play his game, but she also held a very powerful bat. It was powerful enough to hit a home run. The ride back to Long Island was long and boring. The apartment she was going to rent in the city was going to be available at the end of the week. She plugged her IPod into the dashboard and sighed, as she heard Sade's sweet voice fill the air.

It was from another time in her life. Sade was hot, and her romance with Rashaun while he was in law school, was even hotter. As the memories flooded her senses, her face emitted a deep glow. They had been the inseparable couple, the one that love songs were made from. Their love was going to last until the end of time, and with that, a shuffle to the graves six months apart. She lived to feel him, touch him, and inhale everything that was him. He adored her with his eyes, and would tell anyone who was listening, that she was his queen. He even went against his mother's wishes for him, and that was a big thing in Rashaun's life. After his mother found that he wasn't giving Kim up, she had no other choice but to accept her. In time, they became friends, although with guarded feelings. Then there was Derek, Rashaun's best friend, tempting her into a world that would blow her senses. It was the kind of sex that in a lifetime, she would never experience. It was the kind of sex that Rashaun could never give her. Bit by bit, he kept wearing her down, telling her about a feeling that so very few in the world had ever felt. Kim, you are a go getter. Come into this world with me," he beckoned. Eventually, her love for Rashaun was not enough to keep her in his bed. The grass on the other side looked so much greener, and the flowers so much larger and brighter. A seed was planted in her that she needed to see grow.

One night in a hotel room, she succumbed to the mystery. She surrendered to the pain and the pleasure he gave her. And, oh yes, it was good. It was mind blowing, and even earth shattering. It was a feeling she felt that the price of love was well worth paying for. For those brief ten minutes, her body shook in an orgasm that went back to slavery days. The high she felt back then was totally unbelievable. After all of this time, the glow on her face was now gone. She had grown into an uptight, rich black woman, driving back to Long Island, a place she didn't want to go to. For the first time in many years, tears flowed from her eyes. She battered the steering wheel with her fist, as the car inched up to 80 mph. That night, she thought she had gotten what she wanted. It was a turning point in her life. She thought that so much more of this world was now opened up to her. A few weeks later, after Rashaun had left, her phone began to ring, because the most beautiful girl on campus was now available. The dates became a blur, and so did the penises. They offered their souls to her, but that wasn't enough. The few times she saw Rashaun on campus, he was never looking her way. She wanted to reach out to him then, but she also wanted to see the beauty the world had to offer. Finally, she thought that she had seen enough, and wanted to go back to her one true love. He was nowhere to be found. He had disappeared with the winds of time.

In the meantime, she had found that her beauty could be used to get her anything she wanted. Yes, she used her beauty to climb the ladder of success. Even at the height of her accomplishments, with a crowd screaming out her name, she still felt so alone. She had it all, but still felt that she had nothing. She frantically searched for him in the crowds, and looked desperately into blank faces, but he was gone. He had completed her. She had given him up for a life that was now over. Finally, she realized that satisfaction was not just with the body, but came from the spirit. Rashaun had made her spirit whole. They had become one, and together, their glow lit up their world. Oh, what would she give up to have that glow back. The zeroes in her bank account would be thrown away in a minute, if she could spend a night, even under a cardboard box in the city, just to be with him. She knew that her only choice was to get that glow back again. Without it, she felt that life was not worth living.

Chapter V

*A*ndria held Emerald's hand, as they walked from the car into the apartment building. She held a shopping bag in her hand with a present in it.

"Mommy, is Aunty Paula going to have any more babies?" Wisdom asked Andria.

Andria looked at Wisdom, not knowing where that question came from, "I don't know. Why do you ask? "

"Don't know that, either, just curious, I guess. Are we late, because I don't want to miss the clown and the face painting."

"We are about thirty minutes late, but I don't think we will miss anything. We are operating on black people time."

"What's black people time?"

Andria was glad the elevator opened when it did, because she was not in the mood to explain black people time to Wisdom. She rang the doorbell to the apartment, and waited for someone to answer.

Paula opened the door.

"I see you made it." Paula said, as Andria and Wisdom walked inside.

"Do you honestly believe that I would miss my Godchild's birthday party? Hi there, Chance," Andria said, picking up the boy as she started kissing him.

"Hi, Aunty Andria! Is this for me?" He asked, pointing at the bag in Andria's hand.

Andria handed him the bag. "Yes, it is."

"Chance, go and put the present in your room." Paula said.

"Can Wisdom come too, Mommy?" Chance asked.

"Yes he can, but don't make a mess of your room."

The boys ran off in the direction of a blue and white door.

"As you can see, you are one of the early ones," Paula said.

Andria looked around the apartment, and her eyes settled on a young woman watching T.V. in the living room. She looked inquisitively at Paula.

Paula walked with Andria over to the young woman seated on the couch. The woman was wearing tight fitting jeans and a pink blackfunk T-shirt. Her long Indian hair extended to down to her lower back. She got up when Andria and Paula approached the couch.

"Andria, this is Eva, Chris's girlfriend." Paula said.

Andria extended her hand to shake Eva's outstretched right hand. As if on cue, Chris came out of the bathroom that was located only a few feet from the living room.

"What's up, Andria?" he said, as he came over and kissed her on the cheek.

"Everything is good." Andria replied, "And you?"

"I'm good, just started working with the post office last week. It's a lot of training." He said, taking a seat next to Eva.

"That's good. In this recession, jobs are hard to come by these days. Everyone is laying people off."

"You are right about that, I was out of work for almost a year, before I got this one. I thank God I did."

"Come with me, Andria. Let's go and give Jim some help in the kitchen. He must be pulling his hair out in there."Paula said to andria.

"Talk to you later, Chris."

"Don't make Paula work you too hard." Chis said.

"Well, you know I would have her do the same for me. That's what girlfriends are for." Andria answered and as soon as Chris and Eva was out of ear shot, Andria turned to her friend. "What's going on?"

"Chris has calmed down. At first he had a problem, when Jim moved in with me, but gradually he accepted it. He has always been in his son's life, and once he realized that Jim wasn't going to take his place, he stopped being an ass."

"To the point that you invited him and his girlfriend into your apartment with Jim?"

"Jim never had a problem with Chris. It was Chris that had the problem with Jim. Now they both are cool with one another. I think Chris looks up to Jim as a father right now, and they both are taking Chance to see the Yankees on Friday."

Andria kept shaking her head. "I don't believe this."

"I think once Chris saw that Jim wasn't there to take his place, he was able to see Jim for who he is. And once that happened, they were cool with each other. Of course, as you know, it didn't happen overnight."

"Remember Paula, I was at the other end of those late night phone calls. I guess we both have been so busy, that we haven't had a chance to talk."

"Well, I assume something happened when I stopped getting those phone calls."

They walked into the kitchen, as Jim was pulling a tray from the oven.

"Hey baby, you want me to help you with that?" Paula asked.

"Please Babes, I have been cooking a long time, even before you were born." Jim said, while struggling to take the tray out of the oven.

"Is that why you burn everything you try to cook?"

"Andria!"

"I'm staying out of this one. Paula, you want me to go and make the punch?" Andria asked, heading toward the refrigerator.

"How did you know?"

"Because, every time you try to make it, it comes out like syrup. And believe me, these kids already get enough sugar."

"Okay, I admit I'm a little heavy on the sugar. The jug is in the top cabinet," Paula said, as she covered another big foil pan, filled with BBQ chicken."

"I guess that's my cue to leave the kitchen."

"Honey, check on the boys in the room." Paula said.

"Yeah, I'll do that."

"So Andria, what's been happening with that house shopping you guys been doing? You found anything? I hope that you guys buy something with some land space. These boys need a lot of room to run around."

"Girl, let me tell you, looking for a house in Brooklyn is a job in itself. You would swear that we weren't even in a recession, by the high prices these people are selling their houses for."

"Recession what, the landlord just added two hundred dollars onto our rent last week."

"Rashaun's office rent went up, too. I don't know, everyone is raising their prices and no one has jobs."

"I heard it's even worse in Florida. At least house values in New York didn't drop the way they did in the sunshine state."

"Well, the real estate lady called yesterday, and we are going to look at some places over the weekend. Rashaun is very excited about this end property we plan on seeing Sunday."

"Where is Rashaun?"

He tugged the long wild weed, until its roots separated from the ground, dumping it in a small pile next to the head stone. He had been there for almost an hour, pulling each and every weed out from the bed. On the side of the grave were four small piles of weeds. He opened the small white kitchen garbage bag he had brought with him, and dumped the weeds into the bag. Once he was finished, he removed the cream colored surgical gloves from his hands and dumped them into the bag, along with the weeds. Finally satisfied, Rashaun stepped back and took a look at his mother's grave. He missed her so much. The grave was the only place where he felt physically attached to her. She had always been his biggest support, as well as his biggest critic, and biggest fan.

It had been five years since she was shot in the church and died in his arms. He continued to replay that day in his head. She had taken a bullet that was meant for him, a mother's ultimate sacrifice for her son. He didn't even get a chance to even say goodbye to her, because the bullet had lodged directly into her forehead, killing her instantly. Her death occurred on the biggest day of his life, the day he got married to Andria. Such a tremendous tragedy happened on what was to become such a happy life with Andria. But yet, he missed his mom. She was a fighter, and she taught him how to fight. Whenever he was knocked down, she taught him to get up and fight. Rashaun was her diamond, and she was never going to let anything happen to him, and with that came her demise.

Rashaun did not visit her grave after her burial in Pineville Cemetery, in Brooklyn. He did not want to accept the fact that she was gone, and was unwilling to make peace with the departed. He would use every route possible to stay away from the streets close to the cemetery, sometimes turning a fifteen minute trip, into a forty-five minute excursion. He was unable to accept the fact that his bright light in darkness had been extinguished forever. It wasn't until two months after her death, when she came to him at midnight. As was her way, she spoke to him in a tone fit for a little boy.

"Rashaun, stop this foolishness. Put on your clothes and come here," she said, as her voice and body became part of the air he breathed. Once he was dressed, she took him by the hand, like she used to do when he was a boy, and together, they drove to the cemetery. At midnight, the cemetery was closed, so he scaled the fence. She led him to her grave, and once he got there, he wept. In the middle of the night, while holding his mother's hand, he wept like a child. His body was now shuddering, and his nostrils became congested. He pulled at her to let him go, but she wouldn't loosen her grasp. She continued to hold onto him, just like the way she used to, when he was a boy growing up in Barbados. After she had caught him doing something he was told not to do, she would beat him, and then walk him home. He would cry, but not for a second think about letting go of the hand that was guiding him home. That same hand that had walked him to school and picked him up afterwards. That same hand had walked him up the aisle to make his first communion, and was always there to pick him up off the ground, on countless times when he had fallen.

"Thank you, Rashaun. Thank you so much." With tears in his eyes he looked around, puzzled that the wind was now his mother. His look was a questioning one, on the matter of her thanks to him. He believed that it should be the other way around, that he was the one who didn't get the opportunity to thank *her*.

She then continued speaking. "You were my light when I had a physical body, but now, you are even a bigger light in my spirit. I cannot see you physically anymore. I only see your spirit, and it shines so brightly. Now, you and Andria have come together to create another light, that has illuminated the world. In love, you both have created Wisdom, and his light is brighter than both of yours, because you both have come together to make it that way. In the afterlife, there are no bodies. We only see you both as light. Go on now with your life, knowing I will never leave you. Even though my physical body is gone, I'm still here by your side, and will be, until it comes time for you to join me. Get up Rashaun, and don't cry for me anymore."

Rashaun pulled himself up from his mother's grave. Dusting his pants off, he wiped the tears from his eyes. Suddenly, as magically as she appeared, she disappeared into the wind that had formed her. He looked at his mother's grave once more, and made a mental note to return there on Sunday. Even though he couldn't see her anymore, he felt as if she had once again slipped her hand into his, and they were now walking out of the cemetery. When he got out of the cemetery, he looked at the car parked on one of the side roads. He stared at it, but didn't go any further. Instead, he held on tightly to his mother's hand, and they walked all the way home. As he walked with her, they sang songs that she used to teach him as a child. They reminisced about his childhood, and laughed about all the licks and kisses she gave to him. In the wee hours of a Brooklyn morning, Rashaun let go of his mother's physical body, and accepted her eternal spirit. By the time he arrived home, his tears were replaced with an eternal smile, and their love was once more joined with their spirits.

He went into the bathroom and cleaned himself up. As he did every night, he entered his son's room and kissed him, and whispered in his ear his love for him. He then walked into his own bedroom and slipped into the bed.

Andria, as if feeling him for the first time, muttered something, questioning where he was. Then, he whispered, "I love you" and she squeezed him tightly, as she snuggled up next to him.

"I love you, too." He whispered gently. "Thank you."

Tomorrow, she would not remember what transpired on that night in Brooklyn. But Rashaun smiled, because his soul was now transposed forever.

Chapter VI

*K*im watched the lone figure, a long distance away from the beach. He was swimming across the tide, and his body floated effortlessly in and out of the water. She was a good swimmer too, but would never dare to venture out that far into the water. Raqueen was in front of her, playing with the maid and her six year old daughter. As Kim continued to watch the swimmer, seventy-five percent of the people around her were staring at her, wondering who she was. She had not been to Coney Island beach in a long time.

"Who wants a hot dog and French fries?" Kim asked.

"Me, Mommy, with lots of mustard." Valencia said, without lifting up her face from the bucket she was now filling with sand. She was wearing a cute one piece purple bathing suit.

"Me, too. I want lots of ketchup on mine," shouted Raqueen

"Okay, guys. I will be right back." Kim hadn't had a Nathan's hot dog in years, and as she made her way from the sand to the boardwalk, memories of her and Rashaun going on the rides in Coney Island, flashed through her head. She shook her head, as if by doing so, the memories would disappear. As good as Kim looked, her walk was even more sensuous. Each step wined and dined the earth underneath her feet. Each movement showed that her natural beauty was equally shaped by her workouts that were second to none. Her long natural hair, cascading on her shoulders, only epitomized her beauty. She walked like she had it all, and she did so without exception. She joined the line behind a man who appeared to be there with his wife and child. For a minute, the man forgot that he wasn't a bachelor anymore, as he hungrily feasted his eyes on Kim.

"John, we are here!" The woman said, jolting her man back to reality.

"Sorry, Susan. I thought I saw someone I knew back there."

"And Obama is my brother. Here, hold your son." She handed the man the boy who was shirtless.

"I don't do this often, but I had to come over and tell you how beautiful you are."

"Thank you." Kim said, without looking around.

"Are you here by yourself?"

"No."

"Yeah, who comes to Coney Island by themself? I'm here with my sister. Are you ever going to turn around and look at me?"

"Why?"

"To see the handsome man you are talking to."

"You are that confident?"

"Got to be, to approach you. Do you know how many men here want to talk to you, but are afraid to approach you? Even a lesbian chick would be quick to approach you."

"But, you are not like all the other men?"

"Been turned down before, and I ain't afraid of that. Would love some eye contact, though."

"Next!" One of the men behind the counter shouted in the direction of Kim.

"George, you haven't changed at all," Kim said, as she walked to the counter to place her order.

George followed quickly after her, asking "You know me?"

"Yes. And I'm sure you know me, too."

"If I have ever met a beautiful woman like you, I would never forget you. You are absolutely stunning." George said, racking his brain to figure out how the woman knew him.

"You can tell all that without even seeing my face?"

"The whole world can't be wrong, and boy, is the world looking at you."

Kim turned around, and for the first time George saw Kim Rogers, up close and personal. Now he knew why Rashaun got his head so fucked up. This woman would fuck up the mind of a priest.

"Kim, Kim, Kim."

'Why are you saying my name as if it's a bad word?"

"It has been for me, a very long time."

"Then maybe you should leave now." Kim said, as she started walking back to the beach.

George stood there, watching Kim walk away. He had never played Russian Roulette before, because the winner is always the biggest loser. He slowly pressed his feet into the ground, daring them to move. The girl he came with must be pissed as hell right now. He had told her that he was going to get them both hot dogs, French fries and a soda. He couldn't recollect how long ago that was. He stared after Kim, and watched as the earth came up to meet her body. A woman so beautiful shouldn't have it all together like that. Slowly, he felt the pressure in his feet loosen up as he started to contemplate how fast he could run to her. He looked back at the people waiting in line at the Nathan's hot dog stand. He should forget about

Kim, and go and stand in line and wait for his food. The trigger was pulled back and the gun was fired, but there was no bullet in the chamber.

"I'm sorry, Rashaun." George said, as he relented and ran in the direction of Kim.

Fish came out of the water and walked past the pudgy looking man, caught up in the rapture of one of the most beautiful women he had ever seen. He had seen attractive women in Jamaica and in the U.S., but this one was definitely cut from a different cloth. She was standing there effortlessly, and her delicate face with her sensual curves, made his blood boil. He quickly turned away, and walked to the cheese burger café on the beach. He reached into his pocket and pulled out the clear plastic bag that held ten dollar bill. He hoped that a bottle of water didn't cost more than ten dollars. He then took his place in the back of the line.

"Hello, there."

Fish kept his eyes on the slowly moving line. He felt a slight touch on his arm, and he turned around. A white girl, wearing a white tight fitting T-shirt that stopped just above her navel, gave him the most inviting smile.

"You are an unbelievable swimmer. I saw you way out there. You move so effortlessly in the water. I'm a good swimmer myself, but I wouldn't dare go out that far."

"Thank you, it really wasn't that far."

"You are very modest. Do you live around here?"

"No, I live in Carnasie. What about you?"

"My girlfriends and I took the train from Manhattan. I haven't been in Brooklyn in years."

Fish looked at her and was puzzled. His cousins had taken him into Manhattan, and it was only a short ride over the Brooklyn Bridge.

"I know, Manhattan is right over the bridge," she said defensively.

"By the way, my name is Jessica."

"You can call me Fish."

"Are you serious? Your name is Fish?"

Fish laughed. "No, that's not my actual name, it's my nickname."

"Oh." She said smiling.

Her smile lit up her face, creating an energy that Fish felt throughout his whole body. It brought him into her world, whether he wanted to be there or not. In the back of his head, he heard the warnings from his wife in Jamaica. Now, Fish, subconsciously moved away from her.

"Got a long swim back."

Jessica lifted her pink eyebrows. "You are going back in the water?"

"Yeah, I ave to swim back."

"Swim back, where?"

"To my ouse"

"You are Jamaican?"

"Yeah, Montego Bay."

"That is so cool."

"Yeah, I miss it."

"How long you been in this country?"

"A month now."

Jessica looked at Fish, as if she had made a discovery in her science class. All because she had taken a dare from her friends, and went up to talk to Fish. They all had said that he would be unresponsive. Even though she had only briefly flirted with black boys in High School, she had never really dated one. Instead, she had settled for the average white boy. But this summer, after graduating from college, she decided that she wanted to try something new.

"When you going back?"

"Got a three month visa."

"That's really cool. I have always wanted to go to Jamaica." She didn't tell Fish that her girlfriend had recently come back from Jamaica. Her girlfriend had told her about smoking some weed, and getting her ass worked on by a dread. Jessica looked at the ripples on Fish's stomach, and admired it, because it was so meticulously sculpted. She envisioned herself running her fingers over him, as he ran his fingers through her long blonde hair. She knew that the sisters had it going on, but she was no slouch, either. She had full rounded breasts, and a Kim Kadashian ass. Many brothers had holla'd at her, trying to get into her cream puff, but the attraction wasn't mutual. Now, standing next to Fish, she could feel a little moisture gathering in her panties.

"Got to go."

"You got a phone or something?" She asked, taking the time to feast her eyes on his long lean body. "I'm sorry you don't have anything on you. I could see that."

"Got a home phone. I can usually be reached after 10:00 p.m."

Jessica whipped out her cell phone from her tight jean shorts, and took the number Fish gave to her.

"Think your friends are trying to get your attention." Fish said, looking over at three white girls, who were now waving their hands wildly.

"What you doing tomorrow?" Jessica asked.

"Don't know."

"Maybe we can go out and get something to eat. There is a great restaurant, called Negril. We could hang out there."

"Where is it?"

"Manhattan."

"next." The man behind the counter shouted. "We don't have the whole day."

"Talk to you later, Jessica." Fish went up to the counter and ordered a bottle of water.

"Later." Jessica said, and walked back to her group. They hounded her with questions, as they all walked back to the shoreline.

Fish walked back to the beach, passing the pretty woman who was talking to the dumpy looking man. The man shifted his weight constantly, as if he was unsettled about his thoughts. Fish could definitely understand what that guy was going through. He knew that a woman like that could be very intoxicating. Intoxication makes you do foolish things. He remembered his pursuit years ago, of a pretty girl in his homeland. Lucy-Ann was the most beautiful girl in the fifth grade, and every boy in the school wanted to go with her. Not only was Lucy-Ann pretty, she was also smart. In the morning before school started, there would be at least ten boys lined up, waiting to see if they were going to be chosen to carry her bag. Carrying Lucy-Ann's bag gave you the opportunity to talk to her, and everyone got to see you walking and talking to Lucy-Ann. After weeks of standing in that line, sometimes even holding an umbrella in the rain, Fish was finally chosen. With a big smile on his face, Fish walked proudly with Lucy-Ann. On the way to the school, there stood a large wall, where the big waves from the sea splashed against it. Over the years, many people had drowned, when they tried to dive into the water from there. Fish's parents had warned him never to try jumping into the water from up there. A big sign was even posted, that stated that no diving was permitted into the sea from the top of the wall. Fish remembered telling Lucy-Ann that he could do something that no one in the school had ever done before. Most of the time, Fish wore his swim trunks under his school clothes, because he used to go and help his uncle, by the bay after school. Now, this was his opportunity to show Lucy-Ann that he was better than every other boy in the school. As soon as they reached the wall, Fish blurted out that he could do something that no one else in the school could do. Against her objections, he placed his books down, and handed her back her book bag. Fish saw two people in a boat waving to him to get off the wall, but he was determined to prove his point. Ignoring all the warnings, Fish jumped off the wall. When he hit the water, he was all smiles. All he had to do was pump his legs up, to signal to Lucy-Ann that he was okay. As soon as Fish's head broke the surface, a large wave took him under, forcing him to hit hard up against the wall. Immediately from the impact, his right foot tore open, and his right hand broke. That's what caused the severe   pain he felt, before he lost consciousness. When he woke up, he was in St. Mary's Hospital. Fish no longer took chances like that anymore. Although he enjoyed the challenging swims, he didn't dare venture too far from the shores.

Fish dove into the water and came up a short distance from the shore. Slowly, he began the breast stroke, swimming back to Carnasie. The water felt good against his dark skin. He swam effortlessly, as he took long deep breaths, mindful of not over exerting himself, as his body continued to slice the rapidly moving water. He didn't think about the distance he had to go, and instead, felt the peaceful serenity of the ever meandering water. Fish hadn't been idle since landing on American soil. He had gone to the court and obtained the records of the case against his brother, Paul. He also learned a few things about the man who shot him.

Rashaun Jones was an attorney, engaged in private practice in Brooklyn, New York. He was married to Andria, and they had a son named Wisdom. They were currently residing in an apartment in the East Flatbush section of Brooklyn. Rashaun worked six days a week, and he sometimes attended church on Sundays, with his wife and child. He and his wife shared one vehicle, a green Mercedes Benz ML 320 truck. Fish's job didn't give him much time to learn everything about Rashaun, because, he arrived at work at 7:30 a.m., and left at 9:00 p.m. Sometimes, he returned home so exhausted, that he was unable to call his wife in Jamaica. The weekends were the only time that he had some free time, and that was only when they didn't call him in to work to do overtime. Fish thought about different ways to kill Rashaun. Maybe a mugging, as he walked home from work. He also thought about breaking into his office, tying him up, and slitting his throat. Most of all Fish wanted Rashaun to know who was killing him, and why. He wanted Rashaun to feel the pain he felt, when he lost his only sibling. Fish had never taken a man's life before, because he believed that every man had a right to live his life, no matter what kind of life it was. He had come close to death himself, in a few instances when he was attacked and had to defend himself, but he never went over the line. This was un-chartered territory for him, but he was willing to do it, so that his brother's soul could finally rest in peace. He didn't know how he was going to kill Rashaun, but he knew that it had to be done.

Chapter VII

*T*his was a total waste of time!" Rashaun yelled, throwing a stack of papers down on the table.

"Daddy, are you mad?" Wisdom asked. His brown eyes were now focused intently on his father's raised brows.

"I cancelled a meeting with a client for this!"

Sweat was running down Andria's face. She placed her bag down on the table, and went into the kitchen. As if on automatic pilot, she prepared a sandwich for Wisdom, and poured a glass of apple juice to accompany the meal.

"Wisdom, go sit at the table and eat." She said.

Rashaun had gone into the bedroom, and Andria quickly followed him.

"Rashaun, I'm so sorry, but when the real estate lady called and said she had this great deal, and that we needed to see it immediately, I jumped on it."

Rashaun sat down on the bed in his boxer's and wife beater's T-shirt. Andria stood in front the mirror, wearing only her black bra and panties. The temperature outside had just hit 100 degrees, and the AC that was pushing out cool air, wasn't up to the task of cooling off the room.

"It is so hot in here. We definitely need a bigger AC."

"We need a house. This one bedroom apartment is too small for us." Andria took off her bra and floated a dress over her head. "Wisdom, are you finished?"

"Not yet, Mom," He yelled from the kitchen.

"I'm taking him to the park." Rashaun said, as he slipped on a pair of Phat Farm shorts.

"This Real Estate lady really pissed me off today. The house was divided into small boxes. Can you even fit a king sized bed in the master bedroom?"

"Not as far as I can tell."

"And they were asking in the high fives! This is unbelievable. We have been looking for a house for over a year now, and all the houses we have seen so far, have problems. I'm not going to buy a house with no yard. This real estate lady better not call me again. She already knows what we want. Damn! I feel so much like a failure."

"Andria!" Rashaun gently called out, and walked over to her and hugged her.

Andria buried her head in his chest. "You don't ask for much, and all you asked is that I take care of this, and I failed."

"Stop it." Rashaun said, wiping a few tears that were rolling down Andria's cheeks.

"You were so angry today." Andria said.

Rashaun kissed her on the cheek. "Baby, I wasn't angry at you. I know what it's like dealing with Real Estate people in New York. They don't listen to you. All they are thinking about is their commission. They will sell you a toilet, if they could get away with it."

"I didn't want to waste your time."

"You didn't. I needed to get out of the office, anyway."

"Are things getting bad at work, Rashaun, with the recession and everything? I could always get a part time job."

Rashaun led Andria to their bed. "Don't even think about that. We are doing well financially. We are not rich, but we are good. You need to spend the time with Wisdom. I will handle the bills."

Andria shook her head. "If I knew then, what I know now, I would never have gone into social work. There is no money in it."

"Yeah, well at least you have a job. There are lots of people that don't even have that."

"I know, and everyone is blaming Obama, like the poor man is supposed to put a gun behind the corporations and make them hire people."

"Obama will be okay, he got big ass Michelle to take care of him."

Andria pushed Rashaun away. "I can't believe you talking about the President and the First Lady like that."

"Like what? Like a man and a woman? You do know that they are a man and a woman first, before they are President and First Lady."

"It's a weird feeling, talking about the President's sex life. It's like talking about my parents having sex. It's uncomfortable."

"All I'm saying is that Obama got to be tapping that big phat ass."

There was a knock on the bedroom door.

"Come in, Wisdom." Andria said.

Wisdom walked into the room and sat between his parents. Rashaun ran his hands through Wisdom's hair. "Want to go outside?"

"Where, Daddy? Where are we going?"

"Where do you want to go?"

"To the park, so I can skate."

"Then the park it is. Give me a minute to talk to your mom, and I will be right out."

"Okay, Daddy I'm going to get my skates. Can I watch TV while I wait for you?"

"Yeah, go ahead."

"Kim is back." Rashaun stated, as he walked over to the closet to change his clothes.

"What?" Andria's legs suddenly felt very heavy.

Rashaun took a T-shirt from off the shelf. "She stopped by the office the other day."

"And you're just now telling me that?"

Rashaun slipped the T- shirt over his head. "Baby, Kim isn't important."

Andria got up off the bed. "Yes, she is. Every time this woman comes around, she is trying to destroy us, and you know that!"

"The only way anyone could destroy us is if we let them. There is no way I'm going to let Kim hurt us. I promise you that."

"What does she want?'

"She didn't say. She said she wanted us to be friends."

"And you believed that?"

"No, but I don't have time to think about what Kim has up her sleeve. Whatever she comes up with, I think our marriage can withstand it. I have total confidence in what we have here. Neither Kim, nor anyone else, is going to destroy it." Rashaun finished dressing, and came back on the bed to kiss Andria.

Andria shook her head. "I don't like this. This bitch has something up her sleeve. I don't trust her, and I don't want her around my family."

"Andria, it's not that serious. She said her husband died, and she is in New York. Maybe she's here to take care of some business and she'll leave."

"Then, why did she come and visit you?"

"Don't know, and don't care. We have nothing for each other."

"I swear, if this bitch does anything, I'm going to kill her."

Andria's eyes were unblinking. Rashaun was certain that she meant every word she had just said. He opened the bedroom door.

"Be back in an hour. Let's go, big man."

Wisdom ran quickly to the door.

There was a hurricane underway. The wind was blowing the trees down, as if twenty years of growth was now unimportant. The houses were shaking with promises to become heaps of nothingness. Everywhere you looked, there were people screaming, and animals scurrying for shelter. The policemen were on the streets, trying to maintain a level of stability in the growing mayhem. They were pulling on people, holding onto trees, and grabbing animals, and anything else they could put their hands on. George was staring at the phone in his trembling hands. He walked towards the window of his one bedroom apartment. The streets were quiet, as they always were at 3:00 in the morning.

Since meeting Kim, he had not been able to touch another woman. She had been in his dreams day and night, and a vision of her followed him everywhere he went. No woman had ever had that effect on him before, not even the wife he had spent ten years with. He didn't know what Kim had, but he wanted it. And, he wanted it badly. He had picked up the phone numerous times to call Rashaun and tell him about his predicament. But, each time, he hung up the phone before pressing the send button. It had been two weeks since their meeting on the beach. It had been two weeks of hell in an oven. Sometimes he woke up, almost suffocating from the heat, with his body heaving, as he desperately reached out for every little bit of fresh air that was left. He would have to dispense of his wet clothes, and change into something dry. He took one last look at the number, and he pressed send.

"Hi." Kim answered on the first ring, almost as if she was certain that he would call.

"Hello," George replied, his body feeling abnormally calm. The weight of a thousand generations had now been lifted off his shoulders. It felt as though the mouths of starving children in the continent of Africa were now fed.

"I guess you have made your decision." She said, with an apparent deep satisfaction in her voice.

"Don't know what I'm doing, and I don't seem to care why I'm doing it, but you have haunted my shadows. If this is wrong, then I definitely don't want to be right." George said, his voice deeper than usual.

"George, you are taking this way too seriously. What's wrong with going out to dinner with your best friend's ex girl? I don't think you realize it, but Rashaun is married with a child."

"I know happily married. But aren't there rules to this life we live?" George asked

"The only rules to this life are those you cannot afford to break." Kim answered.

"Over twenty years of friendship, for something that is so uncertain."

"George, I know this is difficult for you, but you have to admit, there is something between us. I don't know how far this is going to go, but I'm willing to take a shot at it. I personally don't think Rashaun will care if we got together, and if he does, that's on him." Kim flipped the channels from the remote. She had the deluxe package, and yet, there wasn't anything on cable that interested her.

"He will care, and I am betting with something that is priceless."

"George, what's your last name?"

"Mcleod."

"I'm going out to L.A. on Thursday. I'm going to buy you a ticket, and I want you to meet me at the Jet Blue terminal at 5:00 p.m. on Friday. If you're not there, then you should lose my number." Kim finished what she had to say, and hung up the phone.

George held the phone in his hand, feeling bewildered. He was uncertain whether to put it down, or smash it against the wall. She had called his bluff. In the game of life, the ball is sometimes in your court, and at other times, it's out. The ball was now his to do with whatever he pleased. He went to his "favorites" on his phone. Rashaun's name was right after his wife's name in his program. He clicked it on. It gave him the option to call, text or email. George continued to stare at the options.

"Hey, Rashaun, can we go by the bar later? I got something to talk to you about." He spoke quickly into the phone. There was no reply, because George did not press any of the above options. George went into the cupboard and pulled out a bottle of White Hennessey. He opened the bottle, and took a long swig. His choices were either a weekend in L.A. with Kim, or a conversation with Rashaun. Kim was the kind of woman he felt that the only way he would ever get it, is to pay for it. Kim was the kind of woman who made men's dreams become X-rated. Maybe if he did one weekend and ended it, when he came back, Rashaun would never know. Maybe he could go there with her and nothing would happen. George walked over to the full length mirror in his room, and took another swig of the Hennessey

From where he lived, it only took him about thirty minutes to get to the JFK airport. He would have to go and get a haircut tomorrow, and maybe pick up some new clothes at Macy's. He flopped down onto the bed. He looked over at the phone, and stretched his right hand, reaching out. He then pulled up Kim's contact information. He moved the cursor to the delete button. If he deleted her number, everything would then go away. If he did that, he knew Kim would never call him back. His index finger hovered over the delete button, tormenting him. The hurricane came in full fury now, and this time, it was stronger than ever. He dropped the phone, and grabbed his head with both hands, not knowing whether he had pressed delete or not.

◎◎◎

The bed was shaking, and two pictures had fallen off the night table, as Fish lifted his body up and down.

Jessica's eyes rolled back in her head, as she had her fifth orgasm. Her body was now shaking uncontrollably, as her essence was released. Fish gently lifted her up, and turned her around, so that he could now penetrate her from behind. He was fantasizing that he was with Mindi, and it was feeling so good to him, Mindi always loved when he did it to her from behind. He held her round onion butt in his hands, as he slowly entered her.

"Oh!" She moaned, as he drove further into her. He slowly thrust his dick into her and then withdrew. Again, he repeated the penetration, but this time, he stayed in longer and worked his body back and forth, with short but quick strokes. Then he slowly pulled out of her again. Jessica's blonde hair was flopping from side to side. Fish knew when Mindi was about to have an orgasm, so he continued the buildup, alternating between long and short strokes, some quick, and some slow. And as she continued to build up, so did the intensity of the strokes, until he finally felt her body start to shake. Only then, did he let go of his control, as his own essence flowed freely from his body. Her body started collapsing back onto his, in total satisfaction. When he fell down next to her, Jessica turned to kiss him on the lips, and it was then that Fish realized that he was with Jessica, and not his wife, Mindi.

"You are amazing," She purred, curling up next to his chest.

"Ain't nuthin." He said, running his hands through her smooth blonde hair.

"Let me tell you a secret. We have this impression about black people, especially Jamaicans. Now I can say, that we are far from wrong. Is that wrong?"

"No, we have this impression of white women, too. You know, the ones that come to our island, looking for some action."

"Guess we are just ordinary people, trying to get along. How long are you staying in the U.S.?"

"You already asked me that but about three months."

"My parents have this apartment near Prospect Park, and they usually stay there during the summer. Fortunately for us, this summer they are in Greece. You can stay there, if you like. I'm usually there on the weekends."

Fish thought about the tight quarters that he was currently sharing with his cousin in Canarsie. There was very little privacy, and his aunt's husband was always looking at him suspiciously. This was definitely a good offer. He had also been to some apartments in the white section of Brooklyn, where the people looked at him suspiciously, as if he was about to attack them.

"Is there a doorman?"

"No, it's a two family house my father bought in the early seventies. The other apartment, he rents to a lawyer on Wall Street. You won't have to pay rent or anything."

"What's the catch?"

Jessica had now gotten up out of the bed, and had put on a white T-Shirt. Fish looked at her. She was about 5 feet 8 inches tall, with very little fat on her tight frame. Her breasts were ample and firm, and her butt was definitely right up there, along with his countrywomen. Smiling, she walked back to the bed and lifted the covers off of Fish's body. His dick lay limp between his legs. She straddled herself between his legs, and lifted his dick up with her hands.

"A summer you won't ever forget!" she declared, and with that remark, engulfed her mouth over his dick.

"I like that," Fish said, and knew that he was being 100 % serious. "A summer in New York City, I won't ever forget."

"You like?" Jessica asked, as she lifted her head from his erect penis.

"Yeah, me like a lot."

Jessica straddled Fish's body, and wrapped her legs around both sides of his waist. She slowly went down onto Fish's erect penis. She remembered what she had seen in X-rated movies from the time she was 15 years old, and how she had done this to ten men before Fish. She started to go up and down on Fish's dick, moving rapidly now, as he reached out to grab her waist. Her blonde hair was bouncing off of her shoulders, and her ample breasts were playing with gravity in motion.

Fish did not come to America for this, nor did he come to the U.S. as so many immigrants had in the past, in order to make a better life for himself and his family. No, Fish came to the U.S. to kill a man that had murdered his brother, and that was what he was going to do. As he watched Jessica ride him, he knew that America had so much more to offer. Like the good book says, whatever is given free should always be welcomed and enjoyed. Yeah, Fish was definitely going to enjoy this treat.

Chapter VIII

*I*n the good book, it says that Eve gave Adam a treat, and he took it wholeheartedly because he loved her. George woke up, and even though he thought it was a dream, the woman next to him snapped him back into reality. He had been with many women in his life, and had some unforgettable nights. He looked at the clock on the nightstand, and it showed that the time was approaching midday. Last night, he had been with Eve, a woman from whom all women had come from. If anyone would doubt that the original was the best, he would put up arms against them. Last night, he had an orgasm that didn't originate from his body. It came from the stars. It came from that one particular place they called heaven. Now, he could tell people that heaven surely existed, because he had been there.

He sat up on the bed watching Kim lying next to him, with only part of her face visible. The full length of her body, in all its perfection, was exposed to the elements of the room. He had spent countless times talking to Rashaun about leaving the past alone. The past he had told his friend, was gone. Therefore, he should move on. George never understood what Rashaun was going through. He never for a minute thought that he would meet a woman who would touch his very soul.

A woman to him was a woman. Only tits, pussy, and ass. Once you have been with one, another one won't make a difference. That was his philosophy. It was his way of life, filled with an indefinite string of tits, pussy, and ass. Now, he knew his friend required an apology. The woman lying next to him wasn't just another pussy. She was "it," whatever you considered "it" to fucking be.

Rashaun had tried to explain that to George, but he never wanted to hear about it. It's like a man that never climbed Mount Everest. No one would ever understand why someone would want to climb the highest mountain in the world. Now, George understood when someone says that the person who feels it, knows it. Now, he understood why men jumped off bridges for a woman. Some women touched the body, and others touched the soul. Kim had a way of touching a man's soul. Once a man's soul was touched, his body becomes useless. The soul now becomes the driver, taking them wherever it wants to go. For the first time in his life, George's soul had been touched. Rashaun said that Kim was the devil, and that being with her would be like living in hell. George was willing to live in hell now, and if he ever happened to get out of hell without Kim, he would go to heaven, take a cold shower, and go right back to hell. In the space of two weeks, Kim had done what women have tried for years to do, including his wife. She had opened him up like a surgeon. It was as though he was lying on the table, and she had the scalpel in her hand, with the power to do whatever she wanted.

Kim stirred, and opened her eyes. "You are up early."

"Yeah, that's the teacher in me. Got to get up by six, in order to get to work by 8:15. What are your plans for today?"

"We can go get something to eat."

"Where you want to go?"

'George, you don't want to ask me that. I'm very expensive."

"Hey, you paid for the ticket to come out here, and the least I could do is buy lunch."

"Well, Nicky's has some good food, and it only costs $200 per person," Kim said, unaware that George's mouth had flown open, and now became really dry.

George had gone to expensive restaurants before. He had spent $150 for a fish dinner, and while he was eating it, and paying that price, he wondered if the person who raised the fish, brushed its scales every morning, making sure that there was nothing wrong with it. If the fish was the same damn fish he got at the West Indian restaurant for $10, he was going to ask for his money back. Now, he was looking to spend even $400 for lunch. What in the hell was he going to eat, that after a few days would be passing through his ass, was worth that ridiculous amount of money.

"That's cool." He said, dryly.

"George, you don't have to do it. I can pay for the lunch." Kim got out of the bed and went to the closet. "By the way, they only accept cash."

"I got it," George responded. The last time George checked his account, he only had $750, until he got paid, next payday, which would be on Wednesday. Anyplace else, he would have to take her out with his credit card.

"Are you going to get dressed?" Kim asked George, who was just standing there in his boxers.

"Think you should go in the bathroom first." Reality suddenly came back to George. "You know how you women are."

"George, I think you know by now that I'm not any woman. All I'm going to do is take a quick shower, wash my face, and brush my teeth. I would hope that you would come into the shower to be with me."

"Nope, I refuse to take another shower with a woman. There were too many times that I got stuck holding the soap, without a drop of water on my skin. You guys hog the water."

She walked over to George, and reached inside his boxers. "I think you should come into the shower."

George took one look at Kim, and followed her into the shower.

They took a cab to the restaurant that was located about ten minutes away. Kim wore a pink T-shirt that had," Michael Presley, No Regrets, No Apologies" written on it. Under the writing, there was a man and a woman, locked in an intimate embrace. George wore a blue pair of Kenneth Cole shorts, and an Alfani short sleeved shirt. His outfit was completed with a Chaps pair of loafers.

The Maitre'd, was a short balding white man, nearing the end of his days at any restaurant. He looked up and down at George, and then glanced briefly at Kim. "Where would you like to sit Madam, and will your driver be joining you for dinner?"

"Driver! Do I look like a driver to you?" George wanted so much to make today the man's last day at work.

"I'm sorry Sir, but I was told to expect a woman with a driver, coming here for a delivery. Please forgive me, and drinks are on the house."

"Corner table to the right," Kim said.

"Excellent choice, Madame, will you please follow me."

A serving of warm bread was placed on the table, and their glasses were filled with water.

"Isn't that the actor, Isam?" George looked in the direction of a white man in his early thirties, who had two women with him at his table.

"Yeah, I think so. A lot of celebrities come here. It's the place to be seen."

"And, that's the rapper Little....No it can't be, he is in jail."

"So, what you are going to order?"

George picked up the menu and then he placed it back down. He took out his cell phone, and quickly took a picture. "This is my first," he said, closing the menu.

"This is your first, what?"

George pointed to the menu. "It's in there."

"What's in there?" Kim picked up the menu George had put down, and frantically searched through it.

"They're asking $65.00 for a green salad! I have never seen prices like these before." George shifted his chair from side to side.

"George, you are a fool." Kim said, laughing. "I think I will do the ordering."

"Yeah, I think you should, because this is ridiculous. Why do you come here?"

"I like the food. It's the only place in L.A. where I enjoy eating. Of course, New York has the best restaurants."

"Rashaun...ah." A pale color washed over George's face.

"The elephant in the room," Kim said. "What were you going to say?"

"This is difficult." George looked over at the Maitre'd, talking to an interracial couple, and he looked like he was giving them a hard time, too.

"George, I can't wish anything wasn't so. Things are what they are. You've got to deal with it. Rashaun and I had a relationship about a century ago. It's over now."

"Is it, Kim? Why did you come back to New York?"

"I'm not sure where that is coming from, but my parents live in New York. New York had been my home for over twenty years."

"You told me that your parents lived on the island. Then, why did you get an apartment in Manhattan?"

"Never liked the island."

"Why the twenty questions?"

George's eyes met Kim's. "Because, you are in my blood, and I don't know what to do."

Kim returned the contact. "Stop looking for reasons to end it."

"Life is fucked up. Here I am, having lunch with my best friend's ex-girlfriend, in Los Angeles. I would never think that I would do that. I'm the kind of friend you put a bullet behind their ears."

"George, you are making a mountain out of a mow hill. I will say it again, Rashaun and I are over. I can date whomever I want. You are not going behind Rashaun's back and dating me. We are not hiding anything. If you want, we can finish our meal and I will pay for it, and we can walk out the door and go our separate ways. You don't have to worry about me. I know L.A. pretty well. But if we stay, you have to promise me, that you won't keep having that painful look on your face. I'm going to get up and go to the bathroom now, and when I come back, if you are still here, I will assume that you want to be with me. I have a surprise for you later on tonight." Kim got up and walked towards the bathroom, located in the rear of the restaurant. The actor with the two girls looked at Kim, as if one more was missing from his table. He flashed her that smile that had won him the Emmy last year. Kim ignored him, and kept walking to the bathroom.

George slumped into his chair, much to the dismay of the passing Maitre'd. Kim had given him so many chances to walk away, but he never did. He wanted to, because that would make everything safe. How was he going to look Rashaun in the eyes after what he had done? Would Rashaun ever trust him again? Is the friendship they shared for over twenty years now over?

"Look at Lance, appearing as though he was lost." Tyrone lifted his hand so that Lance could see him.

"Lance can never get lost in a place like this. I think he is just checking out the girl on stage."

Lance walked by the couple and around a table where five guys were sitting and shouting at the girl on stage. There were four empty pitchers of beer on their table. Lance pulled a chair out, and sat between Tyrone and Rashaun.

"You remember when we were like that?" Lance said, looking back at the guys at the table.

"It seems like centuries ago." Tyrone said, as he dipped a buffalo wing into a blue cheese sauce.

"Where the hell is George? George never misses a chance to see naked women." Lance said, pulling out one of the trays filled with Buffalo wings.

"George called and told me he was off to L.A. Some new chick he been banging was giving him a trip." Rashaun picked up a glass of beer.

"A woman, during this recession, is actually taking George to L.A., with all expenses paid? Impossible." Lance dipped a chicken leg into the blue cheese sauce. "Fucking ridiculous."

"I know George, but if he says she's paying, she's paying." Rashaun said.

"I agree with Rashaun, we too old to lie about pussy." Tyrone concurred.

"Damn, who is that?" Lance drew their attention to a woman wearing a red negligee, as she approached their table.

"She is bad." Rashaun commented. "It's your birthday Tyrone, so we will pay for everything."

"That's right man, go for it." Lance added.

"Do you guys want me at this table?" The woman asked.

"Yeah, baby, we definitely do." Lance replied.

"Our friend over here is the birthday boy, so give him the works." Rashaun said, pointing in the direction of Tyrone.

She went over to Tyrone's chair and draped herself over him, her breasts rubbing against his head. "Sorry my friend, Sugar wants some dark chocolate today."

"What!" Lance looked in amazement, as the woman walked around the table to Rashaun. Rashaun was dumbfounded.

"Don't need the money tonight. Tonight, you are all mine." Sugar motioned to two girls walking onto the floor. "My friends, Spice and Cinnamon will take care of you two."

Sugar walked in front of Rashaun and stood there, making him feel as though he was the only one. Then, she slowly started to move her body, gyrating in a slow and sexy way.

"Rashaun, you are fucked." Lance said, with his face hidden from Rashaun by Sugar. "This is one sexy ass bitch."

Sugar gently took Rashaun's face in her hands, and brought it to her ample breasts. She rubbed his face with her breasts. Then, she slowly straddled Rashaun on the chair. Her movements were soft and gentle, the way women have moved for centuries, in order to arouse the passion in men. Her hands expertly traced Rashaun's lean frame, as her body touched him in a way that not even the dead, would be able to stop from having an erection. She took his fingers and put them into her mouth, and slowly started sucking.

Rashaun felt himself rise to the occasion, as the song from his wedding to Andria, played in the background. Even though his mind was fighting not to do this, his body had already thrown the towel in.

In a soft sexy voice, she whispered to Rashaun. "I want you, now."

Rashaun held his head straight up, as Sugar continued her lap dance, using his hard penis that was now being suffocated in his pants, as her own personal toy.

"You do, why?" He managed to say.

"Because, once in a while, we see something that we got to have. And tonight, I got to have you. Don't worry, I see that wedding ring on your finger. How long have you been married?" she asked.

"Five years." Rashaun answered.

"You ever cheated?" Sugar asked.

"No." Rashaun answered.

"Have you ever had someone that looked as good as me come onto you?" Sugar then ran her hand over Rashaun's dick. "I promise you, the sky will open up when you are inside of me."

"I'm sure you are right, but not tonight." Rashaun said.

"Are you saying that you are turning down this pussy?" Sugar stopped dancing for a second. "You got a man at home? That's okay too, because I have been known to turn gay men straight."

"No, a wife." Rashaun answered.

"Then what do you want from me? I'm offering you all three holes, and we can even add another girl to it.

"Been there, done that."

"Not with me, you haven't."

"And I won't."

"You are serious?"

Rashaun looked at her, and his eyes remained unblinking.

She eased herself off of Rashaun's semi hard dick. "I have never! You turned me down, and I was giving you it for free."

The girls, who were working on Lance and Tyrone, now stopped and looked over at Rashaun. He looked like an alien to them. Sugar always gets her man, and that's why she runs this spot. They all aspired to be like Sugar, making $500 and up for just one hook up.

"I won't turn you down, baby." Tyrone said to Sugar.

Sugar looked at him, "Five notes," she said to Tyrone.

"All access?" Tyrone asked.

"For five notes, it better be all access." Lance chimed in.

"Whatever. Let's go." She said to Tyrone.

"Make sure she changes the sheets. Here," Lance handed the girl a hundred dollar bill. "Now, disappear."

She looked as if she just was hit by a big truck. "I didn't do anything!"

"You want me to take it back?" Lance asked.

This time, she took the hint and hurried behind the other girl who was with Tyrone.

"You finally got what you wanted." Rashaun said.

"Yeah, got it all, money and women. I told you guys, I wasn't going to throw these good looks away."

"I heard you are the man that's controlling your stepfather's business."

"Yeah, I'm trying my best. That girl was a bad cheek. Never heard of a stripper giving it up for free."

Rashaun shrugged his shoulders. "Been out of the game for a minute now."

"Andria got you wrapped up." Lance said, taking a long drink.

"That, too. Got nothing out there that I want. Another pussy don't mean nothing to me. I got out of the game because I wanted to. I wasn't forced out."

"I don't think I will ever get out of the game. Married or not, the player stamp stays on my forehead."

"So how come you didn't hit that thing? She was kinda cute."

"Come on Rashaun, you know I'm too cute to be paying for pussy.

We here are dealing with the bottom dwellers. I'm not there, anymore. I'm used to girls pulling up in their Porsches or an LS 400. I don't roll with the Hyundai and Camry's anymore. But, I'm glad you and Andria are still going strong, after five years."

Rashaun smiled. "She can be a pain in the ass sometimes, but every time I wake up and see her face, I know I have been blessed."

"After five years."

"I'm looking forward to twenty more. I hope one day we could retire in the Islands or something."

"What about you?"

"You know my story. Wife and I both like pussy, sometimes we share, and sometimes we don't. Everything is cool, we doing our thing."

"And, Emerald?"

"Emerald is good. You guys must bring Wisdom over a little more often, because they always have so much fun together. My wife is finishing the playground, and it looks like Michael Jackson's Neverland Ranch."

"You get Wisdom in there, and you might have to adopt him."

"I don't think so. That boy of yours feels a lot of love from you all."

"He is precious."

"I know, so is Emerald."

"What happened to that chick that you were all in love with? You don't see her anymore?"

For a minute, Lance's face lit up. "I reached out to her and she wasn't there."

"Yeah"

Lance seemed lost for a minute, "Judy was special. I think that was the first and only time that I have ever been in love."

"Lance, what did you do to the girl?"

"Nothing, man. She made a choice, and it wasn't me. You can't do anything when a choice is made and you are not selected. We had good memories though, and life goes on. She moved out of New York. I'm sure she is out there now, doing her own thing."

"Yeah man, but don't be surprised if she comes back."

"I doubt it."

Rashaun looked over at the stage, and saw that the girl who was with Lance was now dancing for the audience. "Kim is back."

"No, she is not.'

"Yep, she came into my office the other day"

"You got to give her credit, she just don't give up."

Rashaun shook his head, "I don't know about handing out credit, but whenever she is around, shit gets fucked up."

"Did she tell you why she is back? Because, I heard she was going to run for office in D.C., and, that she stands a good chance of winning."

"To be honest with you, I don't know. It's like sitting and waiting for the atomic bomb to drop. You know it's going to drop, but you just don't know when."

Lance motioned for the waitress to come over, "I think you need another drink. This time, we are going to order a Blackfunk, and it's going to get you fucked up."

"Kim will only hurt me if I let her, and I won't let her hurt me or my family."

"Man, if you need money I got your back, and if you need someone taken out, I got that too."

"Damn, Lance, don't tell me you turned into a gangster."

"That old man was into a lot of things."

"Don't get caught out there."

"Let's just say that I'm close to the edge."

"Here comes Tyrone, and he has this big smile on his face, too."

Tyrone pulled the chair out, and flopped down into the seat. "Rashaun, you missed out on some good shit. That woman is unbelievable."

"One's man's loss is another man's gain." Rashaun said.

"Here." Tyrone gave Rashaun a piece of paper that had Sugar's number written on it. "She said she wants to hang out with you sometime. I think you should Rashaun, that pussy was unbelievable."

Rashaun handed the paper back to Tyrone, "I will pass."

"What the fuck happened to the churchman?" Lance said, pushing a drink in front of Tyrone. "After your trial, you were holier than thou. Now look at you, fucking whores in strip joints."

Tyrone sipped on his drink with the straw. "That was some good pussy."

"You said that already." Rashaun replied. "Why don't you just answer the man's question. What happened to the churchman?"

"Okay, okay." Tyrone lifted his hands up. "The church that I was attending was worse than being in a strip joint on a pay weekend. The Pastor on down, were fucking like rabbits. I used to hit a different thing from the church, every week. It started getting me depressed."

"You needed to go to church to find that out? Who do you think are in the church? They are all people like me and you. And if you look around, I'm sure you could find a church that   would sanction even the most perverted stuff you can do." Lance said.

"Yeah, well I didn't know that when I went looking for salvation." Tyrone said, and looked around for Sugar. "I got a conscious. I feel that if I'm going to be a whore, I'm not going to do it in God's house. I felt terrible when I went to church every Sunday and was sinning every Tuesday. There are some really serious freaks in church."

"Now do you feel better?" Lance asked.

"Yeah, I do. I don't feel bad about getting my freak on, then going home to sleep. At least I'm not in God's house, while thinking about how I'm going to tear up that pussy that's sitting behind me." Tyrone said this in a pleading voice, hoping his friends would understand.

"You are the last of the Mohegan's," Rashaun said. "Well, George is back on the market, but that's another story. The way he's been talking about this girl he met recently, there might be a wedding coming up."

"Are you serious? Is he that drunk already?" Tyrone asked.

"Drunk is an understatement. I have never heard George talk about a woman like that before. The way he describes her, it's as though she is pure perfection. He was enamored with her before she even slept with him." Rashaun then placed the empty glass down.

"Maybe its true love, I can't knock the guy. You get caught up in the web. There ain't shit you could do than hope you get fed, or you are not dinner. I had my experience. I don't think I want to go back down that road again." Lance finished the drink in his glass, and looked at Tyrone sipping his. "You're drinking so slowly, and you're going to wind up spending the night here."

"I just finished doing a lot of work. I can't rush my drink down." Tyrone took a longer sip this time.

"Now he is talking shit. Look at his eyes all glazed, as if he's in love or something." Rashaun said.

"Don't go there, Tyrone. You can never make a whore into a house-wife. It might be quicker, turning a housewife into a whore." Lance stated, keeping his eyes focused on Tyrone.

"Why you got to call her a whore?" Tyrone asked.

"He is fucked already." Rashaun said.

"That's fucked up. You got busted open by a woman that busts nuts all day. You need to run back to church, because soon you will need one. "

Lance said.

"Finally," Rashaun said, as Tyrone placed his empty glass down.

"Guess you will be keeping that number?" Rashaun asked, while pushing out his chair.

"Maybe she does house calls," Lance added.

"Yeah, I think I would like to see her in a different environment." Tyrone also got up. He saw Sugar over on the other side of the club, giving a white man a lap dance. He felt like going over there and telling the man to stop, but reality hit him, and he added $5 for the tip, then followed Rashaun and Lance out the door. He still had Sugar's number. He was definitely going to call her.

"So, what you up to later, Lance?" Rashaun asked.

"I got to go check out Donna at the university. You want to come with me?"

"Nah, I will pass. I have got to go and put something together for Monday. I have to write the opening statement for this new client." Rashaun said.

"Seeing that I'm still unemployed after the recession, I'm going home and scratch my balls. Anyone dare to join me?" Tyrone asked, smiling.

"This shit ain't even funny. I should take that damn number from you. You obviously didn't learn anything from your experience with the married woman. Now, you want to go fuck around with a stripper." Lance said. "Be careful she don't charge your ass, every time you bust a nut."

"I know you guys are worried about me. But I'm approaching middle age. Believe me, I know about deadly pussy. Been there, done that. I promised myself that I will never date a married woman again in my life. A lot of people got hurt by my actions. It took me a long time to get over it, too. Now all I want to do is live a peaceful life," Tyrone said.

"With a stripper?" It was a rhetorical question that Lance asked.

"Whatever floats your boat, Tyrone." Rashaun was hoping that they would not see Sugar on the way out. He wasn't in the mood to talk to her, and Tyrone was already on her hook. "Well, I've got to get out of here. I like to be there when my boy goes to bed."

Rashaun and his friends drove off in their different vehicles. Tyrone would make a U-turn onto Flatbush Avenue, and head back to wait for closing time, so that he could take Sugar home.

⊚⊚⊚

Jessica drove onto Flatbush Avenue as if it was the Belt Parkway, weaving in and out of traffic, trying to catch the traffic lights as they turned green. It took about ten minutes to end up in front of a row of garages in Dumbo, which is located underneath the Brooklyn Bridge.

"My father has used this garage for storage for over twenty years. I don't think he remembers half of the stuff he has in here." Jessica said, as they got out of the car. "I usually dump a few things in here every now and then. You told me that you wanted someplace to pack a barrel. How about here?" Jessica asked, as she unlocked the garage door.

"Jesse, you have done so much for me already," Fish said, as he looked into the garage. "It's very quiet down here."

"Yeah, most of the people have already moved their stuff out of these garages, and I think they are going to build condos on this spot. My father has this place until December. I sometimes leave my car here when I go on vacation." Jessica pulled a few boxes out, and reached in to pull out a bag. "I have been looking for this bag."

"You really don't come down here?"

"Nah, whenever I do, I usually have to find someone to come with me. As you can see, this place is very desolate."

Fish looked around, "Yeah, it seems we are the only ones here."

Jessica looked over at Fish. "You don't like this place, either?"

"No, I do. I think this place will be perfect for what I want to do. I think I will take you up on your offer."

"That doesn't mean you could bring girls down here either, because that would piss me off. I understand you got a wife in Jamaica, but I ain't going to share you up here. In America, it's me and you." Jessica's face began turning red.

"Come here, gal," Fish stretched his hands out, and Jessica ran to him. He kissed her passionately on the lips, and slipped his hands under her dress to remove her panties.

"We are…"

"Shut your mouth, gal." Fish said, as he slipped a condom on his erect penis. "Hit the remote to the door."

As the door started to go down, Fish slowly and gently pushed his penis up into Jessica. "Damn, this feels good."

Jessica placed her palms flat onto the garage floor, while standing up straight on her legs. Gradually, Fish increased his thrusts, as he moved in and out of Jessica. Yeah, this was a good place. This place will be perfect for what he came to America to do. Jessica started to scream, as she experienced the first of five orgasms she would have that evening, in the garage. It was of no surprise to Fish, since no one came smashing the door down, saying that he was hurting a white girl. No, this place hadn't seen much action, but Fish was about to change that.

Three hours later, after drinking about four bottles of water from a case that Jessica brought, they decided to close the garage and head out to dinner. Dinner, of course, was on Jessica, like everything else she provided. Fish promised her that when she visited him in Jamaica, he would definitely show her a good time. She might even go fishing with him on his boat. Yeah, and there was nothing like having sex on the beach. Jessica asked him if he promised. "Yes, he said, I promise."

Chapter IX

"You are totally different this morning." Andria said, as she walked out of the Macy's store with Robin. "What has changed?"

"Greg and I are going to save our marriage," Robin declared.

"I always knew that you guys weren't going to break up, anyway. So, give me some info…A vacation, counseling…" Andria seemed at a loss for words.

Robin laughed, "Nobody does that anymore, Andria. Everything starts and ends in the bedroom. This is the internet generation, and we do a lot of self- healing."

"Okay, now you definitely have peaked my interest. What is an internet generation woman going to do to save her marriage?"

Robin and Andria walked through Kings Plaza Mall. "Let's go have a salad at McDonald's. I feel like a kid again, as if I'm about to do something naughty, that only a few people know about."

"Okay Robin, you're freaking me out. I'm excited and nervous at the same time. Now either you tell me, or I'm going to have to choke it out of you." Andria sat down, as Robin went to place the order.

"Do you believe this? The little boy at the cash register tried to talk to me. I'm old enough to take him in and spank him." Robin said, as she placed the food down.

"Maybe he was looking at that bounce in your step." Andria said.

"I think I will go back up and get a Big Mac." Robin said, as she stood to place her order.

"Come on Andria, indulge with me."

"I don't think so. My man is supposed to love me no matter what, but I got to love me, too. I ain't going to be pleased with myself if I have a bubble butt, and a big row of fat around my stomach." Andria took the plastic covering off of the salad bowl.

"You got to lighten up sometimes, Andria." Robin said, and turned around and walked over to the counter.

Andria sipped lightly on the bottle of water, as Robin made her way back to the table.

"Now, he wants me to pick him up after work." Robin said, sliding into the chair opposite Andria.

"Robin, would you stop flirting with the little boy? I could call Paula right now, and she could tell you what to expect."

"Sex, all night long."

Andria looked at Robin with her eyes unwavering. "Now, are you going to tell me what got you so giddy?"

"I know you won't approve, and I don't want you to look at me any differently. I want you to be happy that we are trying to make this marriage work."

"Robin, I will be supportive of anything you guys do. I know how much you guys care for each other."

"We are adding someone else."

"You either are pregnant, or you are going to adopt. I knew you always wanted to adopt a child. I think that's a wonderful idea. You and

Greg have done a great job with my Godchild…"

"Andria, we are adding someone to our bed."

"What! Like another person?" Andria placed her fork down on the table. She had suddenly lost her appetite.

"Yes Andria, and do not start preaching to me." Robin said, biting into her Big Mac.

"Conservative Greg came up with that idea, I bet."

"No, we both did. I think after ten years, we got bored in the bedroom, and that is affecting our relationship."

"Who is she?" Andria asked.

"Why does it have to be a she?"

"Robin, you obviously believe that I'm living under a mat. I know what's going on out there. It is the "in" thing to do these days. Just because I'm not a participant, doesn't mean I'm living in La La land."

"No, we are not taking that route. Women are too grimy, and then the next minute, they're trying to take your man. It's a friend of Greg's, from his job. I already met him, and everything is cool. I'm really excited. Finally, one of my fantasies will come true." The grease poured from Robin's burger with every bite she took.

"You are sure that's what you want to do?"

"Seriously, Andria, do you think a counseling session could have gotten me this excited? And the beauty of it is that I'm not doing anything behind my man's back. We are all doing it out in the open. This is a true test of our love and commitment to each other."

"Why don't you guys just throw bricks at each other to see who gets hit first?" Andria said, nonchalantly.

A frowned appeared on Robin's face, "Now you are being ridiculous. I knew that you wouldn't be able to handle this, but I wanted to tell you, because you are my best friend. Now you are being totally irrational."

"To be honest Robin, I don't see how another man being inside of you will save the boredom in your marriage. I honestly don't see it. But you guys both decided on it, and as your friend, I will always be there for you."

"Andria, I have never been this excited in my life. The only porno I like watching now is those that involve two men and a woman. This is unbelievable. It's like being in another world. How many women can say that they've ever been with two men?"

"I'm sure more than you think."

"I can't wait until Friday."

"We're not young anymore, are we?" Andria asked, looking at a woman on the line who was standing with a little girl, wearing a bow in her hair.

"No, we are close to middle age. There is no going back. What we have to do, we have to do now. Soon, we will be looking at a sunset and wondering where the time went. Hell, I say that right now."

"Well, all I can say is that I wish you luck in getting that excitement back. From looking at you today, I can see that you already did."

"You are not judging me, are you?" Robin asked.

"I honestly don't know what to think. I don't even know what to say. But, we've been friends for donkey years, so all I can do is wish you the best. How is my Godchild?"

Robin exhaled deeply, as if a weight had been lifted off her chest.

"I think she is nervous about her first year in High School. But, I'm sure she is going to be okay. Greg is going to take her to school the first day. He has a way of calming her down."

"The tuition for Wisdom's school just went up by 25%. I don't think these people got the memo that we are in a recession. "Andria said, as she put the rest of the salad into the McDonald's bag.

"I'm glad Eve qualified for the top High School in Brooklyn, because we couldn't afford to send her to a private one."

"You have a smart child."

"Wisdom is not bad, either. The things that he is doing at his age, is nothing short of unbelievable."

"His father does not play where school is concerned. He is on that boy like white on rice. I think sometimes he pushes him a little too hard. But, Wisdom seems to respond very well to it, so I haven't said anything. But if I see it getting out of hand, I will definitely step in." Andria dumped the bag into the garbage container.

"I'm going to really have to work out this week. I'm spending all day in the gym tomorrow." Robin followed Andria and disposed her bag, too.

"Rashaun's been trying to get me to go with him to the gym, but I'm not ready yet. Knowing him, he might be in the gym right now."

"Men and muscles." Robin added, as they walked out the door.

Rashaun rang the doorbell and waited for the door to open. The hallway was painted off white, as was the case with most hallways in Brooklyn. It stemmed from a time when color variations were cost prohibitive. This apartment was located in a building that contained forty apartments, ranging from one bedroom to three bedrooms. The owner, a Grenadian businessman, had recently gone back to his homeland, to live out the rest of his days. The apartment was now being taken care of by his son, Lincoln, who recently married a Trinidadian girl, named Lucy. Rashaun learned all that from the occupant of this apartment, from his best friend, George.

"Damn, you took so long that I thought I would have to use my key." Rashaun said, as he walked by George who was standing on the left side of the wide opened door.

"What are you drinking, my man?" George asked.

"You got any herbal tea?" Rashaun asked, as he took a seat on the couch.

"Yeah I think so. I recently bought a 24 boxed package of herbal tea. This chick I been seeing, watches what she puts into her mouth," George said, walking into the kitchen that overlooked the living room. He opened one of the dark mahogany cabinet doors, and pulled out a large flat box.

"This woman is changing you in more ways than one," Rashaun said, reaching for the remote control that was on the table in front of him. "When do I get to meet her? It seems like you are hiding her from all of us. Is she married, or something?"

"What kind of tea do you want, because there are so many to choose from." George flipped on the stainless steel electric kettle.

"I will have some peppermint," Rashaun replied.

"Good old peppermint, you can't go wrong with that. You want honey in your tea, or are you drinking it straight lately?" George opened another cabinet door, and pulled down an eight ounce bottle of honey.

"I stopped drinking tea with sugar or honey for a long time now, and I'm trying to get Andria to do the same."

"Rashaun, leave the girl alone."

"Nah, I don't stress her about it. Sometimes I actually join her on her junk food cravings, especially with the current and coconut rolls. As a black man getting older, I'm very conscious of health issues associated with us, especially diabetes and high blood pressure. I don't know if I could prevent it, but I could try my best to avoid it, for as long as possible." Rashaun said, as he turned off the TV.

"Got this new CD. Want to check it out?" George asked

"Anything is better than what's on TV these days. It seems like every fucking body has their own reality show. Everyone that is, except for Black people."

George went over to his Bose sound system. "I just got this from this guy that plays for Federation Sounds. I didn't get to listen to the whole thing yet."

"Why, your new woman doesn't like Reggae?" Rashaun asked.

"Actually, she loves Reggae, even though she is an American. She has a whole lot of it on her IPod. I'm trying to get her on the Soca tip, but that's taking a little more time than I expected. But, she has diverse taste in music." George brought the tea over to Rashaun.

"I have never seen you like this with any other woman," Rashaun said, looking at his friend. "This is amazing. I have to meet the woman that flips you like pancakes at IHOP. "

"You right, I have never felt like this before in my life. She is just amazing. She makes me feel like I'm a billionaire."

"You not giving her money are you?" There was genuine concern in Rashaun's voice.

"To be honest, she gives me money. It's like, she has so much money, and she doesn't know what to do with it."

"Did you give her the ring?"

"What do you mean, did I give her the ring? We have only been going out for a short time."

"George, we are in a recession. Any woman that gives you money in these times, you got to put a ring on her finger."

George laughed. "Rashaun, you are hilarious. I recently came out of a divorce. I can't see myself walking down the aisle again so soon."

Rashaun shook his head. "Man, the brothers out there are hungry. Now if this woman is all you say she is, you better do something. She won't be around for long. Someone will snap her up in a minute."

"She is gorgeous."

"So, what's the deal? I'm hearing some hesitation in your voice.

She is married or something?"

George responded " Nothing like that Rashaun. There are issues on the table that I can't discuss right now."

"Don't tell me her man is upstate."

"Damn Rashaun, all the brothers are not upstate."

"I know, George, I'm usually the one trying to keep them from going upstate. I know it's not easy, and some of these poor brothers never got a chance. It's like they are born wearing striped suits."

"Let's not take it there. Have you ever met a woman that is so right for you, it's almost scary?" George asked.

"I don't know what it is George, but no one is that perfect."

"No one is. I would be careful if I were you. Sometimes, when something doesn't feel right it's because it is not. My mother always used to say to listen to that little voice. If that voice says something isn't right, and everything seems perfect, you can bet your ass, something is wrong."

George hesitated, "Or, maybe we are looking for something to be wrong. It's like a person that's feeling really good the whole day, and they are wondering when the bad thing will happen. Why can't it just be a good day, instead of questioning it?"

Rashaun heard the trouble in George's voice. "I think that some-times we have been brought up to believe in the worst. But, sometimes you also have to say "fuck it," and just ride with the happiness wave. You should not go looking for sadness among the happiness. That is an asinine thing to do. Why not just accept the good times? We all deserve some good times in our life, and if it only lasts even an hour, it's good. A day is even better, and a lifetime is ecstasy."

"I hear you." George stated. "Life is simple yet complicated."

"Look at Andria and I. Who knew that our meeting in a club would lead to this? But sometimes, that's just how life is. You just can't put a finger on it. It is forever moving. And I guess that's a good thing, because no one wants to stay stagnant." Rashaun put the empty cup down, before continuing. "When you told me that you were leaving your wife, I told you that you were nuts."

"I remember that. You wanted to kick my ass."

"But you did what you thought you had to do for you. You didn't do it for her, or for me. You did what you had to do for George, and I got to respect that. Now, here you are telling me about a love that you always thought was impossible. If you were still with your wife, maybe you would never have met this new woman."

"Yeah, I know. I still wish the circumstances were different, though. I feel like I'm violating a code or something. I want to be with her, but I think the consequences of doing that would be too much to bear. They say that there is a difference between a rock and a hard place, but right now I can't find the softness, and the stone is bruising me. Did you know that I married Valerie after I graduated from college? At that time, I never thought I would have found someone like her."

"Yeah, I remember."

"And we had some good times. Our marriage worked for a while, until my mind started to go crazy. I knew then that I couldn't stay in it any longer. I was being suffocated. You ever felt like life was passing you by, and you were only a spectator in it? During the last few years of my marriage, I felt like that. It was then that I knew I had to make a decision. A decision that would hurt, but still, it had to be done."

"You did it."

"Sometimes, I wonder if it wasn't just pure selfishness on my part. I left my wife and my son, to pursue a shadow. Did I do the right thing?"

"I think we sometimes get too caught up between what's right and what's wrong. I don't think too many people know the difference. Something that we considered to be totally wrong, can be right, under certain circumstances. If it was even wrong in the first place. Look at the argument over abortion. Most people think it is wrong, unless there are extenuating circumstances. Who determines the circumstances, a preacher or a judge?"

"There you go again Rashaun, getting really deep."

"But, I have a better example. When is it okay to date a friend's ex, or is it ever okay?"

"Damn George, that's a hard one. You got some wine or something?"

George walked toward the kitchen. "My friend left some in the refrigerator last night. I'm not a wine person, but this one was pretty good."

Rashaun got up off the couch. "Where are your wine glasses?"

"Didn't have any of those either, until she brought some. They're in the cupboard, above the stove."

Rashaun reached up to the second shelf, and brought down a pair of blue wine glasses. He turned them over and over in his hand, while admiring them. "George, do you know how much these cost?"

George looked confused, "The wine glasses?"

"Yeah."

"I told you that I have never bought wine glasses before. The only wine glasses I know of, are the plastic ones they give out in the clubs. Or, is it champagne glasses?"

"These cost at least $150 apiece, and that's if you buy them on the internet."

"Are you serious?" George looked as if someone had just pulled his mouth apart. His jaw dropped down completely.

"I don't know who you dating, but that woman must have recently hit the Lottery." Rashaun poured wine in both of the glasses. "And, you don't want to know the cost of this wine."

Rashaun took a sip of the wine, "Yeah, this wine is above top shelf. Whoever this woman is, she doesn't believe in holding anything back. It seems like whatever touches her lips, got to be first class. That begs the question, what the fuck she doing with you?"

"Fuck you, Rashaun." George said, as he took the wine glass from Rashaun. "But you right, she is top class, and she spends money as if she has a never ending supply. I think she is an only child of rich parents. Now, let's get back to my question."

Rashaun drank half of the wine in his glass. "This is some really good shit. I think people have differing opinions on that. Now if you asking me would I date an ex of a best friend, I would tell you no. It's not that I think there is anything wrong with that, it's just that men have this code. It's like the code that you never go back and tell your boy's girl that he is fucking around on her, even though you and her are really cool."

"I think that's different. Only a herb will go and tell his boy that he saw him with another girl. A person like that should get their ass kicked. A guy like that is worse than a bitch. He would need to be put out to pasture."

"I personally think it's the same thing as fucking your boy's ex. I agree, your boy might already have moved on, but it was once his. It's like using the same toilet paper that someone else already used to wipe your ass. It can be done, but who the hell would want to do it."

"Rashaun, you are right, this wine is some good shit. I have never tasted wine like this in my life." George kept staring into the wine glass, hoping to decipher what made it taste so good.

"Well, I know you are not talking about dating one of our exes, because none of them have that kind of money. Unless, you happen to come across something that Lance left behind. And the only ex that I have dated that had money like that, is totally nuts."

"I don't know, man. I think we think of people too much like property. And even though we sell the fucking property, we still want to tell people what to do with the property we sold them. I, for one, think that a man should be able to date whomever he pleases."

"Yeah, I understand that, but it does get a little uncomfortable, when you go to your boy's house, and your ex is in the kitchen, preparing dinner. How would you feel if I was to date Valerie?"

"I honestly wouldn't like it, but it is something that I would have to get over. You and Valerie have a right to date each other."

"Yeah, but it's not about rights. It's about feelings. Why put someone in that position, when there are so many other women out there?"

"Come on Rashaun, there are millions of women out there, but how come you with Andria? You don't want the millions out there, you just want her. Sometimes the world is huge, but sometimes it can seem ridiculously small."

"I understand that, but we all have minds and principles, and sometimes you just have to stop yourself from going in certain directions, even though that route might be paved with gold."

"That's bullshit, Rashaun. Life is too short to live by some kind of bullshit code. We have enough rules that keep us on the straight and narrow. I don't think that adding more codes, is making life any better. I personally feel it's just making the noose around our necks even tighter."

"I hear you. We all got to live our life the way we see fit. I ain't mad at you. By the way, does my Godson still have that show on Sunday?"

"Yeah, I'm going to forward you the email again, because your ass is way too forgetful."

Rashaun finished his wine. "This shit will get me nice real fast. But, I can't have that, I got to get home soon, and drinking and driving is a curse, not a cure."

"I hear you my brother, it's better to leave one behind, than to take one with you."

Rashaun got up off the couch. "What time is it? Andria said she has a surprise for me."

"It's 7:30."

"Damn, I fucked up again. She is going to kill me. She asked me to be home by six." Rashaun hurried to the door to leave.

"You are really domesticated aren't you?" George said, as he followed Rashaun to the door.

"Shit, when my woman says she is going to have a surprise at home for me, I hurry home. It's usually some good stuff."

"Later." George closed the door.

Rashaun opened the apartment door and walked inside.

"Daddy!" Wisdom came running into his arms.

"Hey champion, what are you doing?"

"I am learning Spanish on the internet."

"Yeah, you are. Tell me something you learned in Spanish."

"Hola."

"My son is a Spaniard now. Where is your mom?"

"I think she is mad at you," Wisdom whispered in his ear. "I think she will be giving you a beating."

"Oh, I'm scared."

"Wisdom, who is that in the house?"

"Daddy."

"Are you sure, because your daddy was supposed to be here over an hour ago. Well, tell him I want to talk to him after he is finished with you."

Wisdom looked at his father, with pure confusion on his face.

"Don't worry about it, Wisdom. Your mom is playing with me."

Wisdom started to laugh, "Mommy, you are funny."

Andria came out of the bedroom. "You find me funny, little boy?" She teased, tickling him in the back.

"Hi, Babe," Rashaun called out, as he reached out to kiss Andria.

Andria turned her face, so that he was forced to kiss her on the cheek.

"Can you tell your father that I'm not talking to him?" Andria said, walking back into the room.

"Daddy…"

"That's okay Wisdom, I heard your mom. You can go back and do your Spanish. I am going to talk to your mom." Rashaun said, as he stood up to make his way into the room.

Once he got there, he saw Andria sitting on the bed with a toe scrubber in her hand. In front of her, she had a pink bowl, with steam rising from it.

"Take off your clothes and sit down," She said to Rashaun, while motioning him to the chair.

"Please Andria, not the foot."

"This is my surprise?"

"It is only part of the surprise."

"Does it get any better than this, because this surprise is not very good, so far. Can we do this foot thing another time?"

"Rashaun, you have the roughest feet known to mankind. The bottom of your feet are like Brillo pads, and could cut anything that comes close to them."

"Baby, can we go out to dinner? I feel like eating some Thai food."

"Rashaun, please take off your pants, and your socks, and go and sit down on that chair." Andria once again, pointed to the chair by the window.

"Baby..."

"Rashaun!"

Rashaun took off his pants and his socks. "And why does it have to be a pink bowl? This sure doesn't help my manhood." he said, and sat down on the chair.

Andria brought the bowl and the scrubber, and some other funny looking instruments over to him.

"Lift your feet up and put them into the bowl."

"Ouch!"

"You are such a baby, that I don't know what you will do when your daughter gets here."

Rashaun immediately took his feet out of the bowl, and hugged and kissed Andria. "Why didn't you tell me?"

"Rashaun, will you get your feet back into the bowl?"

"But Honey, we need to celebrate."

"Rashaun, we are not celebrating anything, until we take care of these feet."

"Anything for you." Rashaun replied, and sat back on the chair, and put his feet back into the water. "Are you sure you should be bending like that?"

"Rashaun, please don't start that again. You drove me crazy during Wisdom's pregnancy. I did not become a fragile egg, just because I'm pregnant."

"Okay, I promise I won't treat you like that again."

Andria continued to work on Rashaun's feet. "I think we also might have found our dream home. Robin has this friend that is moving to Florida, and she is selling this beautiful house."

"Sounds great. When do we get to see it?"

"It might be a little bit more than we expected to spend."

Rashaun was now twisting and turning. "Don't worry about that baby, we will make it work."

"You might as well sit back and relax, because we are going to be here for a while."

Rashaun inhaled deeply.

"Did you say something?" Andria asked.

"No babe, not a thing." Rashaun leaned back in the chair and rolled his eyes.

Chapter X

"*D*id you get your man?" Rochele asked, sarcastically. Kim could hear the laughter in her voice, "Yeah, well he has grown overweight with a potbelly, after having five children from five different baby mamas."

"Damn, Kim, I was just making a joke." The laugher had disappeared from her voice.

"Well, that shit wasn't funny."

"My husband wants to know, if you are still running for office." Kim thought about it and said, "I haven't made a decision yet. It all depends on what my husband wants me to do.

"Kim, you don't have a husband. Remember the one you had died in a car accident."

"Yeah, I remember. Now, you know damn well who I'm talking about."

"Damn, Kim, you have so much going for you, and you are going to let a man tell you what to do? This is not about him, it's about you!"

"Rochelle, that's your problem. You are never fucking getting it.

For my whole life, I had money and power, and that didn't do shit for me. Do you think I really give a fuck about being in the government and having all these fucking people suck up to me, while I'm in office? I have only been happy once in my life, and that was only when I was with him. I wouldn't mind sleeping in a shack, if he is by my side. Money doesn't mean shit to me, and I think that you already know that."

There was a pause on the cell phone, "Well, I come from a place where there wasn't enough money to buy even a plate of food at times. And you don't know what kind of living hell that was, and I don't want to go back there. I have taken big dicks too, just so I could get a pair of sneakers to go to work, and I don't want to go back there, either. Now, I'm the one that tells the dicks what to do. I like it this way, and I'm not going back to the fucked up old days."

"Suit yourself. What's been happening in D.C. lately?"

"Not a damn thing, it's still the same old stuff. The five hundred dollar fundraisers, the politicians lying their asses off, just to get into office. Oh, and let's not forget the pretentious bitches running around."

"I hear you, Roche. Well, New York has changed a little. They are doing crazy things to downtown Brooklyn. I heard that the Nets are moving down there. People are still hustling like crazy, because everyone is trying to make a dollar out of fifteen cents, even though they might leave someone else holding the fifteen cents. But the game is the game, and it hasn't changed in a hundred years, so I don't see it changing now."

"New York, New York."

"That's it. Love it, or hate it, ain't going anywhere."

"How is Raqueen?"

"Raqueen is good, but her grandparents are spoiling her rotten. I think that child was a millionaire before she was even born. There are so many trust funds set aside for her, that I think she will need a lawyer just to decipher it all. But, I'm sure my dad has taken care of all that. He doesn't play around with those things."

'So, what are you doing tonight?"

"I'm going by George's place and hang out tonight with him."

"George, who is George? I thought the love of your life's name was Rashaun?"

"It is. George is someone who could be very useful later on. Believe me, everything in life is done for a reason. George, definitely will have his use."

"Well, all I can do is to warn you. I personally think that you are playing with fire, and when you do that, you are liable to get burned. All I can say is that you should be careful."

"I can say the same for you, my dear. That husband of yours is an unlit cocktail. Be careful."

"My house phone is ringing. We will talk again later."

"Bye, Roche." Kim said, as she ended the call.

Kim put a small red and white knapsack over her back. She hung the bicycle helmet on the new Schwinn bicycle she had purchased for $1,200. She had the same one in Washington. She maneuvered herself through the doors, and into the hallway of her building. The short elevator ride took her to the lobby of the building. In front of the building, her Land Rover was waiting. The valet helped her put the bicycle onto the bicycle rack at the back of the truck. For that, she gave him a $5.00 tip.

The ride to Brooklyn was a short one, and even though George lived on a very busy block, she was able to find parking behind a black BMW convertible. She had called George, once she got closer to his building. Now, she sat in the car waiting for him to come down.

George hadn't been biking in about five years. Yesterday, he had to go to his wife's house, and pull his bike out of the garage. He spent almost an hour, just moving stuff out of the way, just to get to the bike. Once he got the bike, he had to clean it. After spending another thirty minutes cleaning the bike, he noticed that one of the spokes was bent. He put the bike into his wife's mini-van, and took it to the repair shop. Of course, once he got there, he found out that there were additional problems with the bike. He left with $60 gone from his wallet for repairs. The store manager had suggested that he buy a new bike, but George told him about the recent plunge in the stock market. The manager then insisted that he trade the bike in, and warned him that the bike was no good. George told him he would rather take his chances.

This bike riding was definitely new to him. He never had been an exercising type of guy. Rashaun was the exercise nut, and on the few occasions he had visited the gym with Rashaun, he had spent most of the time looking at the girls. Just thinking of going bike riding was making him tired. He saw Kim get out of the truck, as he approached her vehicle. She went behind the truck and emerged with her bike, just as he reached her truck. He looked at her bike, then at his, with a look of dismay came over his face. Maybe he should have listened to the bike store manager.

"You ready?" she asked, as she fastened her helmet.

George looked at her helmet, and then at his. "Your helmet looks a lot different than mine."

"Yeah, it is. It's the newest helmet that they are making now. They are very comfortable, and they are breathable.

"I guess they are for true riders."

Kim got on her bike and said, "I won't say all that. I bought it yesterday, because they felt that it was the best one they had in the store. Well, you lead, this is your neighborhood."

"We don't have far to go, only about five blocks, and then, we can go on the Belt Parkway bike path," George said, getting onto his bike.

He rode through the streets of Brooklyn, as if he had paid for their upkeep. Kim followed a full car length behind him. After they crossed the street and rode on Canarsie Pier, they were then able to follow the bike path.

George was sweating profusely, while Kim peddled effortlessly in front of him. He motioned for her to keep peddling, and mouthed that he would eventually catch up. As he approached the hill, he started moving slower and slower, until he stopped completely and dismounted. With sweat covering his entire face, he began to push the bike up the hill.

Kim looked back and saw George struggling to get up the hill. She turned her bike around and rode back to him. She dismounted, and started to laugh at George.

"This isn't funny," George said.

"Let me hold your bike," she said, reaching over to grab George's handlebar. "Now, you take mine, and ride up the hill."

"I think this has more with me being out of shape."

"George, we haven't been riding for fifteen minutes, and I don't think that is the problem."

"Okay, I will try your bike."

George got onto the bike and quickly rode up the hill, and was back next to Kim in a few seconds.

"You are right, the bike does make a big difference." George said, as he dismounted the bike. "I'm buying one just like yours, tomorrow."

"You don't have to get one exactly like this, you just need to get a decent bike. I could buy you one, if you want. It's no big deal."

"Nah, I'm going to buy it. How much does it cost for one like yours?"

"I paid $1,200."

"$1,200 for a bike! Are you serious?"

"And, this is one of the cheaper ones."

"You want me to get you one?" Kim asked.

"Let's walk up the hill. I will get on when we get to the top. I don't think I will have a problem going downhill.

"You want the bike?"

"I don't like this. You do know that I have some pride."

"George, stop being a man with small balls. I'm offering to buy you the bike, because I can. It has nothing to do with your manhood. I'm sure, if you were in my position, you would do the same."

"I would, but that's not the point. It seems that you have been buying me things like crazy since I met you. I have never been in a relationship like this."

"George, you have never been in a relationship with me. Stop trying to compare me with other women you have gone out with. I will pick you up a bike tomorrow. Did you make up your mind, whether you are going to tell Rashaun about us?"

George mumbled something under his breath.

"How long are you going to keep me a secret? I don't like it."

George looked out at the water, feeling like disappearing into it right now. "I'm trying to find a time that is right."

"George, you got to make the time right. If you wait, there might never be a right time," Kim said, getting back on her bike. "It's time to go downhill."

George watched, as Kim rode smoothly down the hill. He wished that his life was like that, just one smooth ride. He was about to do something that might make him lose a friend that he had known for almost a lifetime. But, he knew if he didn't, he might lose the love of a lifetime. He grunted, as he got on the bike, and contrary to Kim's smooth ride downhill, his bike seemed to find every bump that was in the road. When he finally got down to the bottom of the hill, Kim was waiting for him. She looked directly at him for answers.

He didn't know why he said it, but he did, anyway. "Rashaun and Andria are having a goodbye dinner at their apartment on Saturday. You can come with me if you want."

Kim smiled. "Sounds like a plan. I will bring Champagne."

"Finally, we have made it to the top," George said as he looked over at the blue waters in the bay. "Now, I can kick your butt going downhill. This bike flies down a hill."

Kim adjusted her helmet. "I will see you, when I see you, but before I do that, I will give you a head start."

"Normally, I wouldn't do that, but seeing that you have offered, I will take you up on it. But don't be surprised when you see me sitting down, having a sandwich."

"Go, George."

George moved off, slowly at first, but the bike quickly gained momentum on the hill. As he was coasting down, he heard a swoosh sound, as Kim flew past him.

"Damn, I need a new bike. This is embarrassing." George started peddling furiously, before he even reached the bottom of the hill. He looked around, hoping to catch a glimpse of Kim, riding up ahead of him. There was no sign of Kim. He peddled even faster, as thoughts of someone robbing Kim of her bike entered his mind. After a half mile of peddling, he came upon Kim, sitting on her bike, eating a protein bar. George pulled up next to her, totally exhausted.

"You want to try again?" Kim asked.

"Are there people that come and pick you and your bike up, if you run out of steam?" George put the stand of the bike down, and sat next to the bike.

"Nope, we got to ride all the way back."

At that time it became apparent to George that bike riding wasn't for him. "Next time, I will pick the sport."

Andria pressed so many buttons on the phone that someone could have sworn she was practicing for an Olympic sport. Right about now, she hated Rashaun. She hated him, because he had bought her this new phone. After spending years with her flip phone, he insisted that she upgrade to a PDA. Against all her protesting, he switched carriers and changed the phones anyway. Of course, she didn't want unlimited minutes, which she currently had now. She didn't want unlimited text, because she rarely texted anyone. She also spent enough time on the internet on the PC at home, so she definitely didn't want the internet on her phone, too. But she had it, and it was all because she was married to a technology freak. She couldn't wait to get home to tell him that she wanted her old phone back. She sat in the car for almost ten minutes now, trying to send a text message to Robin, telling her she was outside. They had planned on going to the new South African restaurant that recently opened on Fulton Street. A knock on her car window startled Andria. She looked up to see Robin, standing outside the car.

"Did you know how long I have been watching you?" Robin asked, as she sat in the passenger seat.

"Don't even want to know. This phone is going into my bag." Andria dropped the phone into her bag and started the car. "I told him that I loved my old phone."

"Can I see it?" Robin asked.

"You can have it. All I need for you to do is tell my husband to give me back my old phone." Andria took the phone out of her bag and handed it to Robin.

"Andria, this is the best phone out right now. I would love to have a phone like this. Do you know how many things you can do with this phone?"

"Robin, I could barely make a phone call with this phone. I want my old phone back."

Robin pressed two buttons on Andria's phone. "It is that simple, Andria. Two buttons and I'm calling my phone. I'm so glad that Rashaun took that primitive phone away from you. If he hadn't, I think I would have bumped into you, so that the phone would fall and break."

"You would not have done that, would you?"

"Andria, it's not cool to have an 80's phone in the year 2010."

"It wasn't an 80's phone."

"80's, or 90's, who cares? The phone was primitive."

Andria pulled up to the stop sign. "Enough about my fight with technology. What is up with you? How did Friday go?"

"It was an unforgettable experience. We are doing it next Saturday, but with someone different this time."

"It was that good?"

"Yes, it was. I think we need to stop having all these hang-ups about sex. At first, I was a little bit nervous, but with a little wine and some good music, I began to open up. It was unbelievable, having two different man's hands on me at the same time. And that DP thing took me to another level entirely."

"What's DP?"

"Both men are in you at the same time."

"You've got to be kidding me!"

"You did not have your husband and his friend in you at the same time!"

"No Andria, not in your vagina. One is in your vagina, and the other is in your ass."

"Robin, you are making me sick."

"I have a really good husband. We had an unbelievably good time. And I thought my husband was homophobic, but apparently he isn't. Everyone was touching one another. It was as though we all were one. The next morning, I woke up, and my husband's friend was inside me, and my husband was touching me, and we started it up again. I have never had so many orgasms in my life."

"Enough, Robin. I think I've heard enough."

"Andria you have to get with the times, it's like you and that old flip phone. There is so much more out there, you need to open your eyes and live." Robin's cell phone began to ring. "It's Greg."

Andria continued driving, while Robin spoke to her husband. This was new to Andria, and she was having her own difficulties contemplating that life. The woman next to her seemed so different all of a sudden. She always thought she knew Robin, but she was wrong. She did not want to be a prude, but she wasn't comfortable with this conversation.

Robin was smiling from ear to ear, after she hung up the phone. "We are going to do it with another couple this weekend. My husband just confirmed it with them. Andria, this is a whole new exciting world, and the possibilities are endless."

Andria summoned up all her courage, and spoke in an unwavering voice. "Robin, do you mind not talking about this anymore."

"Andria, stop looking at me like that. You are looking at me as if I became the devil or something."

"I'm sorry Robin, but you are not the friend that I have known for all these years. You have always been a woman of reasoning and understanding. I know all of these things are out there, and I'm not telling anyone how to live their life, but this makes me very uncomfortable."

"This is nonsense, Andria. Just because I'm doing something different with my life now, doesn't mean that we can't be friends anymore."

"I agree with you, but all I'm asking is that you give me some time to digest this thing. Remember, I have known you for many years, and this new you, will take a minute or two to get used to. Just give me some time to adjust to it."

"You are right. I didn't think in a thousand years, that I would be going down this road, but as we grow, life changes. I guess that's what's happening with me. To be honest, I don't even know if what Greg and I are doing is going to save our marriage, but at least we are trying something new. I believe that there is a certain amount of honesty, in that everything is out there in the open." Robin eyes searched Andria's face for understanding.

Andria kept her eyes out, looking for the mad Brooklyn drivers. Andria believed that sometimes you have to go out on the ledge for something, but she thought Robin had fallen off of that ledge. She was contemplating that if someone had to go that far to keep something, maybe it wasn't worth keeping. On the road to success, many have fallen to unreachable depths in pursuit of what they thought was something special. She wondered if her friend was able to save her marriage, what kind of marriage she would have now. She had been with Rashaun for five years, and she definitely believed that he was her soul mate, but how far should she go to stay with him?

"I have said it before Robin. I wish you success in keeping your marriage together, whatever way you see fit. In this world, we are all given the freedom to do what we think is right, regardless of the outcome."

"Thanks Andria, we have been through a lot, and regardless of what happens, I always want to know that we have one another's shoulders to lean on."

"This is getting somber."

"Are we that old?"

"We are talking like our parents."

Andria's phone began to ring. "I guess that's what we are becoming."

Robin looked out the window, not paying particular attention to anything. "Yeah, life is changing."

Rashaun had been sitting in the kitchen for over an hour now. In front of him was a cup, with about quarter of the contents remaining. The time was now ten after twelve. He didn't know if she was going to come, but he had to talk to her. He didn't know why he thought she was going to come visit him on this particular night, but something deep down inside her, told him she would. Suddenly, he felt a whisp of cold air enter the room, and he sat up in his chair. He looked directly over at the cup of tea, and he knew she was there.

"I guess I don't have to ask for the tea." Her voice filled the cold room with warmth.

"You always said my head was hard, but I have since learned a few things."

Albertina wasn't a warm body anymore, and when she spoke, the words didn't come from her mouth. Instead, they flowed from the image that was now within her.

"Yes, hard as a coconut, but beautiful, nonetheless. Congratulations on the house, I like it."

Rashaun didn't question how she knew that he had bought a house. To do that, would mean having to question his own sanity, because here he was in the kitchen, talking to his mother, who had died years ago.

"Yes, finally." Rashaun exhaled, powerfully.

"The spirits in the house are good spirits, and they will give you peace. The house has been waiting for you."

Rashaun looked over at his mother. "Mom…"

"Rashaun, certain houses have spirits in them, and those spirits choose their occupants. There are a lot of things happening around you, that you aren't aware of. And sometimes, what you see isn't what's really there. Sometimes, frustrations from the human life get transmitted to the spiritual world. I have a friend here that has been trying to talk to her daughter for the longest time. But the daughter refuses to listen. My friend thought that now that she became a spirit, maybe her daughter would listen. But no, she hasn't. Because the daughter refuses to listen or to feel emotions, and her time on earth will be short."

"But you can't influence what happens here?"

"Are you asking me, or telling me?"

"No, we can't. Only you can take the actions on this earth. We can only open your eyes so that you can see."

"But I can see."

"Rashaun, remember when you told me about an accident that occurred when you were about seventeen years old? You and a group of your friends were standing on the sidewalk, when a car jumped the curb."

"Yeah I remember, and that girl was killed."

"You said that everyone, including the girl, saw the car coming, but she didn't get away. You wondered if she panicked or something like that."

"Yes."

"Well she didn't panic, and she wasn't in shock. She was looking, but she wasn't actually seeing, because she was looking through a recorder. What she saw wasn't really what was happening in front of her eyes. What she saw, was something that happened a long time ago, therefore she was lost. There are a lot of lost people out there Rashaun, with their eyes open, but they aren't seeing things clearly. For a long time, that was true of you.

Now, you are actually seeing and are aware of things."

In all his years of college and law school, he was never privy to information like this. Rashaun was now getting a lesson in life from his dead mother.

"Mom, how do you know about all of this?"

"Rashaun, do not question the giver. Instead, accept what you have and leave the rest behind. In life there will always be two paths you can take. One comes from the heart, and will fill you up and satisfy you wherever you go. The other path without love will fill you up, but you will never be satisfied. The one without heart will make you a slave to its demands, and at the end of your journey, you will have accomplished everything, but gain nothing from the experience. We come into this world with nothing, and we leave with nothing. When you leave this earth, you won't be taking your law degree with you, or that house you are about to move into. You'll leave behind Andria and Wisdom, as well as the other two that are on the way."

"Are you saying that I'm going to have three children?"

"Rashaun, a question will come up about your possessions, and your answer will determine the direction you will take for the rest of your life. I have said enough. Enjoy your dinner party and remember we possess nothing but our soul." Albertina said, as her image swept over Rashaun in the form of a chilly wind.

Rashaun sat back on the kitchen chair, and his right hand played with the cup. It was just like his mother to leave him confused. Even though his mother did not get past the sixth grade, her wisdom in life was unmatched by any written words. He remembered once her predicting that it would rain, when all the weather men said that it wouldn't. He then stopped listening to the weathermen after that, and instead, would call his mother to find out what she thought. The only thing she couldn't predict was snow. Rashaun got up from the chair and turned the kitchen light off. He needed to get some rest, because for the next few days, he knew that Andria would

Chapter XI

*R*ashaun stared at the computer screen as though transfixed by the images. He had lost almost $20,000 since the recession began. The down payment and the closing costs of the house he was buying, were now reduced. He had to take some money out of his savings and added this to his investment money in order to purchase the house. Rashaun didn't like touching his savings, but the poor stock market performance didn't leave him a choice. He looked at a snapshot on the computer screen of his savings, the Wisdom College Fund, his investment portfolio and his IRA's. The money he had hoped to make by selling his Condo had also been reduced by about one third the value of what it was worth. While his financial picture wasn't bleak, it was still much less than he had a few years ago. Yet, he still felt blessed, because while so many people were now losing their possessions, he was about to buy a house. Some of his friends weren't making out as well as he was in the recession, and he recently had to lend George $5,000. Andria was now putting the final touches on the apartment for the dinner party. The catered food was delivered about five minutes ago, and Andria lit the warmers under the trays. They had used Erica's Catering House to cater the food for the dinner party. Erica's catering house was founded by a Guyanese woman and a Jamaican couple from Brooklyn. Rashaun believed in supporting businesses in the local community, and that was something that was drilled into him by his mother. She always said that a community that supports itself will always be able to take care of itself. The knock on the door was persistent but light, and he knew that it had to be Wisdom.

"Come in, Wisdom." Rashaun said, turning to the door.

Wisdom opened the door and entered and said, "Mommy said it's time to get ready."

"She did?" Rashaun said, pulling his son closer to him. He squeezed Wisdom and rubbed his head.

"Are you ready for a party?"

"Yep, Mom said she invited kids, too."

"I'm sure she did. Why aren't you dressed?" Rashaun asked.

"Mom said you have to give me a bath and then I will get dressed. She said my clothes are on the bed and you can help me get dressed.

Rashaun looked towards the door. "Do you think we could sneak into the kitchen and get some food first?"

"No Daddy, Mom said we can't eat until the guests arrive."

Rashaun lifted Wisdom up and put him on his shoulders. Wisdom's head was hanging over Rashaun's back.

"I guess it's time to give you a bath then," he said, while carrying Wisdom into the bathroom.

Andria was relieved when she heard the shower start. She knew that her husband, would wait until the first guest arrived before he decided to get dressed. She had checked both bathrooms at least three times to ensure that she didn't forget anything. One of the things she liked about this condo was the fact that it had a full bathroom and another half bathroom, therefore their privacy was maintained in events like these. She had started to clean the apartment on Monday and wasn't finished until Thursday. Rashaun had grown tired of her cleaning, and told her that he didn't think anyone would be eating off of the floor. But Andria had grown up with a mother who believed that cleanliness was next to Godliness, and she wanted to be at the head of the line at heaven's gates. She checked to make sure that all the warmers were on, one last time, and then looked at her watch for the tenth time. According to "black people time," the guests would start arriving at 7:30, and it was now 6:45 p.m. Andria had bathed and taken care of herself, and now all she needed to do was put her dress on. She took one last look at the tables and chairs. They had removed all the furniture from the living room and had set up six tables, each with four chairs. Each table was covered with a white table cloth, and a small vase filled with fresh flowers stood on the middle of each one. Rashaun had connected his MP3 player to the stereo, so that the music would be a mixture of Reggae, R&B, and Andria's favorite, Jazz. Rashaun only cared about the Reggae. She took one last look at the living room, before she headed back into the bedroom to put on her dress. This evening, she was wearing a light green dress that was opened in the back. She didn't have to worry about her stomach, because she was only two months into the pregnancy. It hadn't even been two minutes since she put on her dress, when the doorbell rang.

Rashaun was in Wisdom's room, getting him ready for the party. Andria knew that he wasn't finished, so she went to answer the door. Paula had mentioned that she would arrive a little early to help her with the party.

"Hey, Girl," Paula said as she walked into the apartment. "This place looks really good."

"Been working at it. Where is Jim and Chance?"

"Where do you want me to put this?" Paula asked, her bag stretched out in front of her.

"I have cleaned out the closet, so I guess we can put all the bags in there."

Paula opened the closet door and placed her bag on one of the shelves. "Did you really want me to bring Jim and Chance early? They will drive us crazy. Now, what can I do to help you?"

Andria looked at the clock on the wall. "I guess we can start bringing out the drinks from the kitchen."

"Got it." Paula said, and headed towards the kitchen.

"They are on the table. The punch is for the kids, and the pitcher is on the counter."

"I went to a birthday party once, and the people accidentally spiked the kid's punch. The kids went totally wild. I had to run with Chance."

"No, they didn't."

"Couldn't even make that up." Paula returned with a two gallon cooler.

"I already told Rashaun, that the men will drink only wine or beer, since we are not having any hard liquor."

"There are pitchers for each table, so the kids don't have to get up every minute."

"Tea is a big thing these days. Do you have any?"

Andria stopped fixing the table. "I didn't think of that."

"What do you have to boil the water in?"

"There is a water heater on the counter, you think that will do?"

"This is fine. All we need to do is fill it up and plug it in. Where are your tea bags?"

"They're in the cabinet next to the stove."

"Girl, you have a lot of teas."

"Yeah, Rashaun visits China Town weekly. And believe me he has tried each and every one of them."

"I heard my name mentioned." Rashaun came out of the bedroom in slacks and a T-shirt. "Honey, are you telling Paula how great a husband I am?"

"Good evening, Rashaun."

"What's up Paula? Where is the rest of the crew?"

"They should be here in about thirty minutes. Congrats on the new house."

"Thank you. Now I have to deal with my wife telling me to cut the grass."

"You need the exercise." Andria said, placing some plates in Rashaun's hands. "Put them on the tables."

Rashaun looked at the plates and then at Andria. "I thought you already gave me a job?"

Then, the doorbell rang.

Rashaun put the plates back in Andria's hands. "I will get the door."

Andria shot him the evil look, "I'm going to kill you."

Rashaun opened the door. "Tyrone and …." Rashaun was stunned that he was now staring at the stripper from the club.

"Sugar" Sugar answered, helping Rashaun with his memory lapse.

"Sugar, do you have a last name?" Rashaun asked, as they walked in.

"That's not important." Sugar walked in, holding on to Tyrone's hands.

Rashaun gave Tyrone the *"what the fuck did you do that for"* look.

"I told Sugar that you were having a dinner party and she became really excited. She couldn't wait to meet Andria." Tyrone said, ignoring Rashaun's glare.

Rashaun shook his head, wondering why strippers always had to dress like strippers. Sugar was wearing a pair of very short red pants and a tightly fitted white armless blouse with high stiletto shoes.

"Hi, Tyrone," Andria said, as Tyrone kissed her on the cheeks.

"Andria, this is my friend, Sugar." Tyrone acknowledged Sugar who was now standing behind him.

"Nice to meet you." Sugar extended her hand to Andria and Andria shook it warmly.

"You guys are the first ones here so you can pick a table. Tyrone, you know Paula, right?" Andria could feel Paula's eyes boring into Sugar.

"Hey, Tyrone and Sugar!" Paula waved at them.

"How is the family, Paula?" Tyrone asked.

"The family is good. They should be here any moment now."

"As I said guys, pick a table and you can have a seat. I will be right back." Andria said, following Paula into the kitchen.

As soon as Andria shut the kitchen door, Paula was on her. "Who the hell is Tyrone with? She looks like a straight up hooker."

Andria looked at her as if surprised that Paula would ask her that question. "Why are you asking me? Tyrone is Rashaun's friend, not mine. I don't know who that girl is."

"Did she know that she was coming to a dinner party? She is dressed totally inappropriately." Paula said, as she leaned over the sink.

"Paula, we did not issue a dress code for this evening, so people have the right to dress however they want to." Andria said. "I think we have brought everything out, and now it's time to go and wait for the guests."

"I still think she looks like a hooker. What the hell is wrong with Rashaun's friends? With all the women that are available out there, they can't find a decent one. You saw the one that Lance went and married. She is nothing but bones. And George, he left is wife to be a slut, and I can't wait to see who he will bring. Thank God you have decent girlfriends. By the way, why isn't Robin here?"

"Robin called a few minutes ago and said that they are on their way over." Andria said, as she turned around to leave the kitchen.

"I have been so busy with Chance, that I haven't had the time to talk to Robin lately. How is she doing?"

"Why don't you ask her when she gets here?"

"Okay, I guess you don't want to talk about Robin."

For a minute, Andria seemed flustered. "I guess I'm a little tired since I've been up the last few nights, preparing for this party."

"Andria, take it easy, everything will be okay." Paula hugged Andria around the shoulders.

Andria patted Paula on the back, "Everything is fine, so let's go out there. I think I heard your husband's voice."

"Yeah, I think I hear him, too." Paula said, as Andria opened the door.

They hadn't taken three steps past the kitchen door before Chance shouted, "Mommy!" and ran to Paula. He hugged his mother.

"Aunty Andria, where is Wisdom?" Chance asked.

"If I had to bet, he is in his room playing with his DSI." Andria said, looking around the room.

"Can I go to his room?" Chance asked.

"Go ahead, you know where it is." Andria replied. Andria looked around for Rashaun, and saw him reaching into the cooler that held the beers. He gave one to Jim. The doorbell rang again, and Rashaun motioned to Tyrone to answer it. Andria looked over to see Lance walking in with his wife and son, Emerald. Lance and Tyrone exchanged handshakes, and then Emerald went over to Rashaun. Andria couldn't hear what they were saying, but she was sure that Emerald would make a bee line to Wisdom's room. As if reading her mind, Emerald did just that. Andria went over to greet Lance and his wife.

"Congrats." Lance said, and he reached out and kissed Andria on both cheeks.

"Thank you. I see Emerald has disappeared," Andria said, as she exchanged a kiss on the cheek with Laura, Lance's wife.

"Donald said you guys were able to find a house with land space in Brooklyn. I'm sure that wasn't easy." Laura said, as they walk toward the tables.

"Girl, that definitely wasn't easy. The Real Estate people in this city do not listen to you." Andria said.

"I will leave you guys to talk. I see your husband over there, Andria. I'm going to speak with him." Lance exited without waiting for a reply from either of the ladies.

Lance walked up to Tyrone and Rashaun who were now talking to one another.

"I see you brought the wife along this time." Tyrone said, as Lance approached them. "You guys are such a happy couple."

"Tyrone, please don't throw stones. Your house is not even made of glass, it is constructed of tissue paper. What the fuck you still doing with that hooker?" Lance said, as he accepted a beer from Rashaun.

"She is not a hooker, she is an exotic dancer." Tyrone answered.

"Didn't you tell the girl she was going to a dinner party?" Lance asked.

"Yeah." Tyrone answered.

"Then, why the fuck she dressed up like she is going to work at the strip club?" Lance looked over to where Sugar was sitting by herself, holding a bottle of water in front of her.

"Tyrone, Lance got a point. Your girl is dressed as if she is going to work." Rashaun added.

"I told her about it. But she said that's what she feels comfortable with," Tyrone replied.

"Whatever man, where the hell is George?" Lance asked.

"He called a few minutes ago to say his girl is running late. Almost everyone is here, except for my father and Andria's mother." Rashaun said, looking around the room.

"Forget about that, they just walked in." Tyrone s looked over at the two older people that had entered the room.

"Hey, your father seems to be really caught up with Andria's mother. Your Pops must be coming out for one more round." Lance's eyes were now focused on Rashaun's father and Andria's mother. "Your Pop's looking good, too. Is he going to the gym or something?"

"Yeah, he started going with me a few months ago. I don't know why." Rashaun said.

"Lance is right, and the reason is right here. It's Andria's Mom," Tyrone said.

"You guys are just talking shit. I got better things to do than to stand here and talk shit with you guys. I'm going to go and do my hosting duties." Rashaun walk away from his friends, and went to talk to Lance's wife who was in a group, along with his father and Andria's mother.

As he was talking to them, Andria came up to the side of him. "Excuse me, but I need to talk to Rashaun."

"The wife calls." Rashaun said, and bowed out of the group.

"This is beautiful, Andria, I know my son had nothing to do with this." Rashaun's father said, as Rashaun and Andria walked away.

"Pops, you know him too well." Andria replied, before turning to Rashaun. "Baby, I think we should start eating now. Everyone has a table and Paula told me that her family is hungry."

"I know Baby. I was trying to wait until George got here." Rashaun replied.

"Did he call?" Andria asked.

"He called earlier to say that they were running late." Rashaun said, looking at his watch again.

"I understand that Honey, but we can't keep everyone waiting just for your friend. I know how you feel about him, but I don't think that is fair to everyone else." Andria said.

"Okay, let's wait five more minutes. If he doesn't call and is not here by then, we will proceed." Rashaun said.

"Okay, only five more minutes. I need to get another spoon from the kitchen." Andria said, and walked away from Rashaun.

"I will change the music." Rashaun headed towards the stereo set that was located in the corner of the room.

"Hey Rashaun, Sugar wants to hear some Rap." Tyrone said, coming up next to Rashaun as he was adjusting his iPod.

"Rap? Tyrone, you better tell your girl that this is not that kind of party." Rashaun said.

"Don't you have a little JayZ or something?" Tyrone asked. "She's feeling kind of funny, like she don't belong in here or something. I told her the people in here are cool people."

"I'm about to start this dinner, so she is going to have to wait." Rashaun said, returning his attention back to his IPod.

"You're not going to wait for George?" Tyrone asked.

"It's almost 9:00 and I can't keep these people waiting any longer." Rashaun said.

"You right, and I am hungry. I didn't eat because I know you used Erica's catering service so I came here with an empty stomach." Tyrone said. "George is never late for food, so that chick must have him by the strings."

"Don't know, but the show got to go on." Rashaun said. "By the way, you seen that girl he's with?"

"Nah, I'm starting to believe that she doesn't exist. Maybe George has gone on the other side, because it's not like him to hide the woman he is with." Tyrone said, looking at the door.

Rashaun looked at Tyrone as if he had just fallen out of the sky. "George could go a lot of places, but the other side of pussy doesn't exist for George. It's like a big black hole."

"Just bull shitting you. I see Andria and Robin are serving some things, and hopefully it's food. Later." Tyrone made his way back to Sugar who now seemed a little agitated.

Rashaun turned down the volume on the stereo as some soulful jazz came out of the speakers. He went back to his table which was located at the top of the room, close to the six foot sliding glass door that led out to the balcony. Seated at his table were Andria and Wisdom. Rashaun's father and Andria's mother occupied the table directly in front of them. On the right side of the parents sat Robin and her husband Greg, and their daughter. Lance and his wife and Emerald occupied the table next to Robin. Tyrone and Sugar completed the seating arrangements. There was only one table left empty, and that was intended for George and his girlfriend.

Andria look at her watch as Rashaun returned to the table.

It was a hint too obvious for Rashaun to ignore. He had tried his best to stall, waiting for George to arrive, but he couldn't do it anymore. When he got to his chair, he didn't pull it out to sit down and instead, remained standing.

"Family and friends, I would like to take this opportunity to thank you all for coming. As you guys know, we have been looking for a house for a long time. I'm very happy to announce that we have found one in Brooklyn. So, our next dinner party will be held outside on the patio. We will be moving at the end of the month." Rashaun look at Andria, before continuing. "I would also like to announce…"

Suddenly, the doorbell rang. Rashaun waited, as Robin's husband who was located the closest to the door, went to answer it. Rashaun definitely wanted his friend George to hear what he was about to say. George stepped in and Rashaun smiled, as he saw his best friend shake Greg's hand. By this time, everyone's eyes were following Rashaun to the door. It was then that Kim stepped into the room. The look on Rashaun's face was priceless, and contorted into rage and anger. Rashaun looked at Andria, whose mouth was now ajar. The room that was once peaceful and celebratory now held the intensity of a sudden silent explosion.

Lance was the first to respond to Rashaun's movement. He saw his friend move his chair back. Immediately Lance stepped in front of Rashaun, to block his path to the door. Robin was watching Andria's reaction and when Andria stood up, so did she. She intercepted Andria, as she went towards the advancing couple of George and Kim.

"Mommy, Daddy!" Wisdom screamed.

"*You!*" there was anger and hatred in Rashaun's voice. It was unclear who the "*You*" was directed towards. Lance felt the trembling in Rashaun's hands as he pulled his friend into the bedroom. Robin took Andria out onto the patio, barely having enough strength to restrain her friend. The bedroom door slammed shut, and the patio door was now closed as well.

"Damn, that woman makes me look ugly." Sugar said to a steaming Tyrone.

"I would like to kill that bitch." Tyrone replied.

"What the fuck did she do? This whole room changed when she walked in. She got to be one bad bitch." Sugar replied. She watched Kim walk towards Andria's table, with her hand clasped tightly around Raqueen. Kim placed the bottle of champagne on the table, and then she and George and Raqueen took a seat at the empty table.

"I'm sorry about the interruption, but my son and daughter in law will be back soon. In the meantime, the food is self -serve, and now I would like everyone to take their plates, and please go ahead and help yourselves." Mr. Jones said, as he got his plate and walked toward the food located at the side of the room.

Rashaun was pacing in the room, while Lance sat on the chair watching him.

"He is my best friend." Rashaun said and the tension was now evident in his voice.

"I don't think George is thinking clearly. I think Kim got him whipped. This is not the George we know." Lance sadly replied.

"I don't care. George knows how Andria and I feel about Kim. He had been with us throughout the whole ordeal we had with her. What the fuck has changed?" Rashaun angrily cried out.

"I hear you." Lance said

"How could he do that to me? I would never do that to him. We go way back. I've known George since elementary school. We fucked girls together! This man is the keeper of my darkest secrets. And for him to do this to me! I swear if I had a gun I would have shot his ass." Rashaun continued pacing. "This is my apartment. You, as a friend do not bring poison to your friend's house."

"Rashaun, I don't think George is in his right mind." Lance said.

"Whatever state of mind George is in, I want him out of my fucking house." Rashaun said.

Lance got up out of the chair and walked over to Rashaun. "I don't think you should ask them to leave. I think you need to send Kim a message. You need for her to see that you are not rattled by her antics. Like it or not, you are in a war with your ex, and she just gave you a blow. It's up to you now to show that you can take it without being knocked out."

Rashaun just shook his head. "I'm not in a war with Kim. I don't give a fuck what's happening to that bitch. Kim doesn't exist for me."

"Rashaun, I'm sure Obama felt the same way about the right wing. He wasn't fighting them, but they are fighting him, because he didn't acknowledge that he was in a war with them. They are about to derail his presidency. You cannot keep ignoring blows that are hitting you on the head. Those blows eventually will give you a concussion, and that isn't good." Lance put his hand on Rashaun's shoulder. "You got to go out there and show Kim and George that you will not fall down."

"I don't know if I could do that, Lance." Rashaun said. "I feel that I was just betrayed by Judah. Why didn't he tell me?"

"I think he was afraid of your reaction." Lance answered.

"So, instead he chose to bring her in my house and rub my face in it!" Rashaun yelled, as his voice became more emotional.

"Rashaun, answer this honestly, do you have any feelings for Kim?" Lance asked.

Rashaun looked up at the ceiling. "To be honest with you, I had feelings for her for a long time after we broke up. But as time went on, and things happened, the feelings became less and less. Now, I can honestly say that I don't have any feelings left for her. I just want this woman out of my life for good. I think her soul purpose is to make me unhappy, because she cannot find happiness for herself."

"You don't get it, do you?" Lance asked.

"Get what?" Rashaun looked confused by Lance's words.

"This woman is not fighting to destroy you. She is fighting for a love that she felt had gotten away. This woman wants you, and she is willing to do anything to have you." Lance said.

"But, I don't want her. I'm happy with my wife and my son. The last five years, I have experienced some of the best things in the world." Rashaun replied.

"Do you honestly believe that Kim knows that or even cares?" Lance asked.

"Lance, I told you I don't care about that." Rashaun replied.

"Well, I would suggest you start caring about that. Because, the only way to deal with Kim is to know her next move, and you move before she does. I do business every day, and most of the time I'm playing with my life. What keeps me breathing is being able to anticipate my enemy's moves, and be ready to deal with them."

"Lance, I'm not fighting a war!" Rashaun shouted.

"Yes, you are!" Lance replied, his voice equally as loud. "Rashaun you keep expecting Kim to go away, but she won't. Not as long as she thinks that you have something that she wants."

"Lance, there isn't a damn thing Kim could do for me to go back with her. I'd rather jump off the Brooklyn Bridge before I would do that." Rashaun said. "Now, can you go and get those motherfuckers out of my house, unless you want me to do it myself."

"Okay, I will do as you say, but you might be ending a friendship."

"The friendship ended from the time he walked in here with her."

"I could bring him in here for you guys to talk through this thing."

"No, thanks, just get them out of here. They wanted to make a point, and the point was made. Now, I have a dinner to finish."

"Alright."

As was expected, all eyes were on Lance when he came out of the bedroom. Lance turned to look out onto the terrace, but the curtain was drawn and he couldn't see Robin and Andria. He saw Kim, George and Raqueen sitting at the last table, and he walked over to them.

"George, let me holla at you." Lance said sternly.

George got up from the table. "What's up?"

Lance looked him straight in the eyes. "You guys got to go."

"What! Let me talk to Rashaun."

Lance stepped in front of him. "He doesn't want to talk to you. He just wants you to get the fuck out."

"I understand this might not look right, but Rashaun got to let go."

"I'm not here to argue with you about what Rashaun should do or not do. I'm telling you, the brother said to get the fuck out of his house and he meant it."

"So, he can't come out here and tell me?"

"Trust me, George you don't want Rashaun coming out here right now. I would suggest
you leave now."

"So, what do I tell Raqueen here?" George looked down at the little girl who seemed totally confused.

"George, it's not my place to tell you what to say to anyone. Rashaun don't want you guys here. Leave now, so that the dinner party can continue. You and Rashaun could get into this some other time."

Kim stood up. "Let's go, George. Your friend doesn't want you here."

Lance looked over at Kim. "Listen to your woman, George."

George turned around to look at the faces in the room, and they were all staring at him. He felt like the main performer who had just gotten up on stage, and now they were waiting for his next move. "Rashaun and I go way back. Let me go talk to him."

Lance started to frown. "George, you are missing the point. I'm here because Rashaun don't want to see your face."

"Let's go, Raqueen." Kim said, and took her daughter by the hand as she started walking towards the door.

"Tell Rashaun to get over it. She is with me now." George said sternly, before he turned and followed Kim to the door.

As Lance walked back into the room to get Rashaun, he glanced at the guests. Rashaun's father was busy talking with Andria's mother, and Tyrone and Sugar seemed to be in their own little world. Paula had brought Wisdom to sit with them at the table, and Robin's husband seemed preoccupied with his daughter.

"They left." Lance said, as he shut the bedroom door.

Rashaun turned away from looking outside the window. "Where is Andria?"

"She is still on the patio with Robin."

"I don't think she will want to continue the dinner," Rashaun said.

"You got to convince her to continue it. You can't let Kim disrupt your life like that."

"I agree. I will go and talk to her." Rashaun headed towards the bedroom door.

"Hold on a second." Lance said, as he approached his friend. "Did you see Kim's daughter?"

"No, I was too angry to see anyone but Kim and George." Rashaun responded hesitantly.

Lance shook his head. "I know they sometimes say you can wish a face on a child, but this is scary."

"Lance, what the fuck are you talking about?"

"Kim's daughter is the spitting image of you."

Rashaun walked back into the room and sat down on the bed. "You saw it, too."

Now, Lance looked puzzled. "I thought you hadn't seen her?"

"Kim showed me a photograph."

"You didn't hit it before she left New York?"

"The last time I touched Kim that way was in college. Since then, we have never been intimate." Rashaun rose from the bed.

"This is very interesting." Lance said. "I'm hungry man, and I'm going to get some food. Lance opened the door and went out ahead of Rashaun.

"Don't really feel like eating, but I'm going to get Andria." Rashaun said, as he ignored the eyes that were on him when he exited the room. He made a bee line to the patio, pulling the door back and stepping outside.

"Rashaun, I'm not going back out there." Andria said, as Rashaun shut the door closed.

Robin looked agitated. "I told her that she can't let this woman disrupt her life like that, but she refuses to listen to me."

Rashaun went over and hugged Andria, who was sitting on a white plastic chair. "Baby, I understand how you feel, but they're now gone. Robin is right. If we let them spoil our dinner, then they have won."

"Rashaun, I don't care about who wins. Your friend brought this evil woman into our house, and she's bent on destroying us."

Andria didn't get angry very often, but this time she was totally pissed off. Even though Rashaun didn't appreciate George bringing Kim here, he was more upset at George, than Kim. He believed in the respect code. George had broken that now, over a woman. He had seen the change in George since he started seeing Kim, but he just thought it was new love. It was now very obvious that George had lost control. Now because of that, his woman was in pain. Rashaun didn't like to see Andria like this, and it hurt him deep within his heart. Somehow, he had to get her to go back to their guests and dinner party.

"Baby, we have a house full of people and a five course meal prepared for this wonderful celebration. George and Kim have already gone, and I think we owe it to our guests to finish the dinner. I understand it won't be the same, but we will have a housewarming soon, and believe me, there won't be a repeat of this." Rashaun took Andria by the hand. "Now let's go and finish our dinner."

Andria looked at Rashaun and then at Robin, who remained silent while Rashaun spoke to her. Now Robin's eyes were pleading with Andria to finish the dinner party. "Okay, but can we end it soon?"

"Baby, we will end it as soon as everyone has eaten." Rashaun pulled the sliding door back as Andria rose from the chair.

Robin went ahead of them as they walked back into the living room. Rashaun acknowledge his guests with a slight bow, and they went over and sat at their table.

Paula immediately went over to them. "What are you guys eating?"

Andria looked at her pensively. "I don't think I want anything to eat."

"Andria, if I have to force the food down your throat, you are definitely having something to eat. The baked chicken is off the chains," Paula said.

"I think she would love a plate. Paula, thank you." Rashaun said. "I will join you to get mine in a minute."

"Get ready Andria, I'm going to get your food." Paula turned and walked away.

Rashaun leaned over and whispered in Andria's ear. "Baby, I'm going to get something to eat and will be back in a second."

"Okay," Andria replied, and sipped at the glass of water that was in front of her.

Rashaun walked over to the side of the room where the food was located. He took a plate and started to go down the line.

Tyrone came up behind him with his plate. "This food is really good, and this is my second helping."

"Yeah, I heard." Rashaun replied, with his eyes still on the food.

Tyrone took a few legs of the baked chicken. The chicken had a deep brown coloring. "Is Andria okay?"

"Yeah, she is good, just a little bit shaken up."

"George is a fucking asshole."

"Yeah, he is a dickhead."

"Did you see him? It was like he was in a trance. If I ever get like that over some pussy, please shoot me." Tyrone said, adding some mashed potatoes to the side of the chicken.

Rashaun looked over at Sugar, who was busy taking a bite out of a chicken leg. "What's up with Sugar?"

Tyrone looked back at him and laughed. "You don't think I'm hooked over some stripper/hooker pussy do you?"

"I have seen stranger things, and this evening is a perfect example." Rashaun said, adding some salad to the chicken on his plate.

"If I didn't learn my lesson with Judy, someone should cut my dick off immediately. Sugar is cool to hang out with. That's it." Tyrone said.

"Never underestimate the power of pussy." Rashaun said, and added some green beans to his plate.

"I'm too old for that."

"A man is never too old to get trapped by a female."

"You're right, and George is a perfect example of that. After George left his wife, I never thought I would see the day when he was into just one woman. George was player extraordinaire, and he fell harder than a breadfruit in a hurricane." Tyrone shook his head. "To be honest, the brother looked pitiful. Your ex must have some gladiator shit."

"I feel sorry for the brother. That woman will chew him up and spit . him out."

"You don't think its true love?"

"Kim wouldn't know true love if it went directly into her bloodstream."

Tyrone took a little bit of the mixed salad. "Let me get back to Sugar. She's looking kind of bored there. By the way, Sugar wanted me to ask you something."

"What?" Rashaun asked, with irritation now evident in his voice.

Tyrone stood still for a minute. "Relax Rashaun, she just was talking crazy."

Rashaun gave Tyrone the look that said "just go ahead and ask me the fucking question."

"She wanted to know if you and Kim had a child together."

"So you told her no, right?"

"I did, but she said to ask you anyway. She thought that the child Kim came in with was a replica of you." Tyrone turned around. "I will holla at you later."

Rashaun leaned over the tray of peas and rice. His hand seemed to be frozen in time. He thought about it again, and he still came up with the same answer. The only way that Kim could have gotten pregnant by him is if she had frozen his sperm ten years ago. He shook his head, thinking that Kim was crazy, but she wasn't that crazy.

Chapter XII

*F*ish hurried up the steps of the subway station exit as if he was being chased by a crazy man with a machete. He had heard about the New York City subway stations and didn't like the experience one bit. This was about the twentieth time he had been in a subway, and his feelings for it hadn't change. The subway was one of the safest means of transportation, but he felt trapped within its winding tracks. The few times he had chosen to sit in the subway train, the journey left him mentally paralyzed as the train rattled along. His feet would shake nervously, and his hands would be filled with perspiration by the time he got off at his stop. He followed the directions Jessica gave him to get to the restaurant in the Village. He had met Jessica a few times for dinner in Manhattan at some popular restaurants, and also at a few holes in the walls. One of them didn't even have a name yet, and they had to wait thirty minutes before they were seated.

The passing clouds had darkened the streets a little, but it hadn't stopped the flow of people entering one of the most culturally diverse parts of New York City. Fish glanced at the numbers on the building, to ensure that he was traveling in the right direction. She had told him that he couldn't miss the restaurant, because it was the only one with outside dining. Fish had asked her how she knew about so many restaurants. She had told him that from the time she was a child, she had been going to them. Her parents rarely cooked, and they were hardly ever home on time to eat, whenever the housekeeper prepared dinner. They would always meet their dad or their mom somewhere in the city to have dinner. Attending college in NYC prevented her from even thinking about turning on the stove, because there was always a new restaurant to go to. She and her friends would eat, study, and sometimes even sleep at restaurants. Money wasn't a problem, so they just enjoyed the social life.

Fish gave up looking for numbers to find the restaurant, because most of the buildings didn't have numbers on them, or the numbers were too difficult to read. After walking about five blocks, he finally saw a restaurant that had chairs and umbrellas outside. Jessica was sitting at one of the tables outside, reading a novel. She saw him approaching, and waved to him, as he continued to walk towards the restaurant.

Jessica was waiting at the front by the time he got to the restaurant. She grabbed his hand and led him to her table. "I thought you got lost or something." She said.

"No, the trains were running a little late." Fish replied, as he took a seat opposite her.

Jessica looked over at Fish. "You look good," she whispered with unwavering eyes.

"Thanks, you always look good." He replied.

"I missed you the past two days."

"Yeah, I know. I have been busy trying to take care of my business before I leave to go back home."

Fish had been following Rashaun for more than a week. He had trailed him from work to their new house. He had followed him and his family to the supermarket, their parent's house, and even to church. He now had a good idea about what Rashaun did and when and where he did it. Yesterday, he sent three barrels back home to Jamaica. He would be home in less than three weeks. Jessica had helped him pick up the stuff for the barrels and had given him the money to purchase some of the goods for his home. He liked Jessica. She was honest and sincere. Under different circumstances, he could see himself in a relationship with her. But he knew that was impossible, because he was still deeply in love with his wife at home. While he saw the possibilities of a relationship with Jessica, he understood that she was just a filler, with advantages.

"I don't want to believe that you will be gone in a few weeks. These last few weeks have been the best ever. I never knew a dare would end up with me falling in love." Jessica blurted out, almost uncontrollably. "I'm sorry, Fish, we said we wouldn't talk like that."

Fish look directly into her eyes. "I understand, and I'm sorry, too. I tried to be honest with you from the very beginning, because I didn't want any complications."

"I understand that. I know you are leaving in a few weeks. I know you have a woman at home that you are going back to. I didn't want to fall in love with you, but it happened. These last few weeks have been the best time of my life."

"I have had a good time with you, too. But…"

"But you are not in love with me."

"Jessica."

"I don't need for you to say it, and I know you will, if I ask you to. But what I feel is about me, not about you. I have to deal with it. I thought this was just going to be an experience, but it turned out to be a lot more."

"Same here."

Jessica reached over and gripped both of Fish's hands. "I don't know what I will do without you. You are a tremendous person. I offer you so much, but you only take what you need. A lot of guys would just run all over me. I respect you for that. My last relationship was with a guy that tried to get as much out of me as possible. He drove away, right after I bought him a new car." Jessica squeezed Fish's hand and continued. "Not you. Even though all my friends told me to expect this and that from you because you are black, is all untrue. They were right about one thing, though."

"What's that?" Fish asked.

"You Island men really know how to work it." Jessica said, smiling.

"Well, I have to admit something, too."

"Is this confession time?"

"I had some misconceptions, too."

"White women want to suck dick all day, and we like to be spanked?"

Fish started to laugh. "Spanked, too!"

"Well I have also heard that Jamaican men don't eat pussy, either."

"You didn't hear that from a Jamaican woman. You must have heard it from an American. What I was going to say before you told me what you thought, is that there is a misconception that you guys do not like spicy foods, but the way you ate the fish I cooked the other day, was totally crazy."

"That fish you cooked was unbelievable. I have to get the recipe to make fish like that. I have never had fish done up like that."

"If you thought that was good, come to Jamaica and have them cook it when the fishermen just come in from the sea. It will make you go crazy." Fish said.

"Heard you guys talking about Jamaica. I just came back from Ocho Rios, and that place is great. My friends and I are planning a trip there for next year." The waitress was a slim red head wearing a black uniform. "You guys want to order now, or do you need more time?"

"I need a lot more time with him." Jessica said, looking longingly at Fish.

"I bet you do. I will be back in a few." The waitress said.

"Thanks," Jessica replied, as the waitress walked away. "I don't know if she was talking about the Jamaican men or the country itself."

"Whatever it is, we need the help in Jamaica."

"When do I get to come and see you there?" Jessica asked, her voice now taking on a very serious tone.

"I don't know." Fish looked beyond her, almost as if he was envisioning his life in Jamaica. He had never been unfaithful to his wife before. Women were never that important to him. He loved the sea and what it had to offer him. He never had to lie to his wife about where he was or what he was doing. They say that what happens in America, stays in America, but now they were talking about bringing it to Jamaica.

Jessica looked deeply into Fish's eyes. "You don't mess around on your wife, do you?"

Fish took a deep breath, "Why do you ask?"

"I thought I had it all figured out and once more, I'm wrong. I could have sworn that you were fucking everything with a triangle in Jamaica. Now I see that you aren't like that at all. It's another misconception about Jamaicans. To a larger extent, black men in general. Let's get back to my original question. I already know that I want to see you after you leave here. I can leave here anytime I have a break from school," Jessica pleaded, her voice now taking on a hint of urgency.

"We will see." Fish said.

Jessica smiled and looked away from Fish. "I have heard that line before. When you leave New York, will I ever see you again?"

"Jessica, you are asking for guarantees. I can't give you that. My life in Jamaica is not the same as it is here. Before we even got together, I told you about my wife in Jamaica, and that remains the same. I cannot tell you to come to Jamaica and we will continue where we left off. I'm a different man there. I love my wife, and we are about to start a family."

"I understand all that. I have put myself in a difficult situation. I don't want to wait for a call from you that never comes. I don't want to come to Jamaica and never get a chance to see you."

"You have been great to me. You have given me more than most of my relatives here have given me. I'm truly thankful and appreciative for what you have done. But, I don't want to make promises to you that I can't keep."

"I understand that, but can you give me something to hold on to? Can you promise me that when I come to Jamaica, you will see me?"

Fish looked out far down the street. A woman was crossing the street with a young child. "I will see you when you come to Jamaica," he promised.

A smile, brighter than sunshine, now lit up Jessica's face. "How much more time do I have with you?"

"I'm leaving in three weeks."

Jessica motioned to the waitress to come over to their table. "We would like to have our orders to go."

"Are you playing me?" George asked. George and Kim were sitting in the kitchen of George's apartment. George had on green and black boxers, and Kim wore a knitted black negligee. George had never seen an outfit like that before, when she walked in about two hours ago. At first he thought she had on a regular T–Shirt, with a long skirt. But then she told him to have a seat on the couch. First, she took off her T-Shirt, and George saw the netted fabric covering her top that had two holes cut out for her nipples. When she took off her skirt, George saw that she was wearing a one piece suit with a section cut out for her vagina. George got down on his knees and he crawled towards her, like an animal, about to pounce on his prey. He didn't know he could get this hard. There he was, in the middle of the living room, lapping between Kim's legs, like a hungry puppy. She took his head in her hands and buried it deeper inside of her, almost cutting off his oxygen supply. She came hard, with a tremendous shudder and then she bent over and touched her toes. George entered her from behind, and in only about ninety seconds, he fell to the floor, totally drained of his body fluids.

Kim looked confused. "What are you talking about?"

"I spoke to Lance last night, and he told me that you were playing me. You were using me to get back at Rashaun."

"Is that true?"

"George, how old are you?"

"You know my age."

"I do. I was thinking maybe you forgot. Why the fuck do you have your friend telling you what someone else is doing to you. Do you think I'm using you? We have been having some great times together. Do you honestly think I'm still going after Rashaun?"

"I don't know what to think. My head is all fucked up. I haven't spoken to my best friend in over a month. My other friends think I'm a dog. I honestly don't know what's going on."

Kim stood up and took the empty glass that was in front of George. She brought both glasses to the sink. She was still wearing high heels, and her walk accentuated every curve in her body.

"Do you want anything else?"

George went over to Kim and grabbed her neck from behind and shoved it down into the sink. He entered her with the force of a hundred angry men. "Don't fuck me." He said, as he continued to drive into her.

Kim adjusted herself so that she could receive him fully and she matched his thrusts with such energy and passion, that it forced George to dig his toes into the floor. He thrust even harder now, while she pounded into him. He slapped her butt, and she screamed for him to thrust even harder. She held on to the ends of the sink, as his movements became rapid. "Fuck me harder!" She screamed. "Let it hurt!"

George put his legs, his back, his chest and every inch of his body into fucking her really good. To anyone looking at them, it would seem that they were hurting each other, but you couldn't tell which one was doing the hurting now, because they were giving it to each other as good as they were getting it.

"I love you! I hate you!" He screamed as he continued to draw all the energy from within himself, to give her what she wanted.

"Give me more!" Kim's body was now building to a crescendo. Her legs were shaking and her fingers were trembling.

Sweat began to pour down George's face and onto Kim's butt and continued down to the crack of her ass. George's whole body felt as tight as a screw in concrete. His muscles contracted quickly, as he felt her vagina grip his penis even tighter. Now, his whole body began trembling as was hers, and with every inch of his last remaining strength, he gave her one hard final thrust, and Kim came back onto him with an equally strong bounce. His semen shot out of his body like a cannon erupting, and Kim squirted for the first time in years. They both fell down on the cold kitchen floor, panting and sweating.

"Rashaun will have to get over you." George declared. "You are mine, now."

Kim looked up into George's clouded eyes and smiled. She got up off the floor and looked back down at him. "Are we going to the movies?"

George looked at her. "Yeah, later, much later. Get me a pillow, because I don't think I can get up now."

"You want me to order the tickets online? Yeah, we should definitely do that. We don't have to go and see that movie."

George shook his head. "No, I want to see "BLACKFUNK." I heard there will never be a movie like it again."

Kim looked down at him. "But George, can you handle it?"

"Like you said, I'm a big man. If I could handle you, I could handle anything."

Kim laughed, as she walked over to George. "Now, I'm horny. You just got me started!"

George shook his head. "Give me a minute," He lied, because he knew he needed a lot more than a fucking minute to recover.

Chapter XIII

*T*hank you, Baby!" Andria said, while staring at the bouquet of flowers that were just delivered to her office.

"You deserve it and a lot more." Rashaun moved the statue, so that he could wipe underneath it. He had taken the day off to do some cleaning around the house and a few other things. "Sometimes I don't think I take the time to tell you how great you are."

"You don't have to say anything, you show me every time you look at me. I feel it all over." Andria's eyes were watery with emotions.

"Since we got this new house, I don't think we have stopped working for a minute. It seems every time you turn around, there is something to do."

"Yeah, and I know I have a big job waiting for me when I get home. Since the workmen came and sanded and painted the walls, there is dust everywhere."

"Don't worry about that. I will take care of it.'

"Rashaun, don't hire anyone to come in and clean, because we can't afford it."

"Don't worry about it. I promise you it will be taken care of. By the way, what time are you leaving work?" Rashaun asked.

"Why?"

"Because, I would like to take my beautiful wife out to dinner," Rashaun answered. "If you don't mind."

"Baby I don't mind what you do with me. But, we do have a son to take care of," Andria said.

"Dad bought a new toy for Wisdom, and he already begged me to sleep over by his grandfather."

"Well, it is Friday. We can go pick him up in the morning," Andria concluded.

"Now, is it okay for me to spend some time with my wife?" Rashaun asked.

"Well, I will be home by 5:30, and then you can have me all to yourself. Maybe we can include a spa treatment, seeing that you are being so romantic. I know it's not your style, but I love massages."

"You know I hate to go to those places. I don't like to see people's hands on you baby, but if that's what you want, we can do it." There appeared to be a slight irritation in Rashaun's voice.

"Just testing you, Baby like I said, we will do whatever you want us to do. It's been so long since we really spent some time together. I miss your touch so much. Did you finish that class you were taking?" Andria asked.

"Yeah, I finished it yesterday, and it was only a one week course. Now I will see if I learned anything."

"They are giving you a test?"

"Yeah, and if I don't pass, a lot of people won't be happy."

'Stop it, Rashaun. You haven't failed a test since grade school."

"I know, but I'm still nervous about it, and right now, I don't want to think of anything but you. Now, I have to go and finish this project and I will pick you up at 5:30." Rashaun said.

"Honey, I will take the train."

"No, you won't. I told you I needed to use the car today, but I'm still picking you up. I will see you later." Rashaun said.

"Bye, honey."

"5:30."

Rashaun finished cleaning the shelf and went upstairs. The guest room was the first room on the left. It was approximately nine feet by twelve feet. Next to the guest room was where Wisdom's room was located. It measured twelve feet by twelve feet and as he passed by, he looked into it and wondered how the room had gotten crowded so quickly. Next to Wisdom's room was his bathroom, and opposite it was their office. The hallway upstairs was painted a light pastel orange color. Each bedroom had a different color. The guest room was off white, and Wisdom's room was painted a faded burgundy color that he had chosen himself. The office was painted green for money. At least, that's what he had told Andria. The office was able to hold three desks. Rashaun's was the cleanest, and Andria's desk was even messier than Wisdom's, even though she promised to clean it up. Rashaun opened the door that led him into the bathroom that was attached to the master bedroom. It held two sinks, a whirlpool, a standing shower and a separate stall for the commode. It had taken him about an hour to clean the bathroom this morning, and the flowers that were now surrounding the tub, were delivered around the same time that Andria received hers at work. He had also placed some scented candles around the tub. He washed his hands, then went in and took a shower. It was two o'clock, and that meant that he had three hours to prepare the salmon he had picked up from the market this morning. As he headed downstairs to start cooking, thoughts of his mom once again engaged his mind. She was the chef, and with her help, he was capable of doing anything in the kitchen.

Now, he would have to do it all alone.

"Hold on." Rashaun said. He then got out of the car and went over to the passenger's side to open Andria's door.

"Rashaun you are driving me crazy." Andria said as she stepped out of the car. The car was parked in the driveway in front of the garage. A garage that Rashaun promised he was going to tackle next summer. Presently, it held all the things that they thought they wanted to keep, but didn't know where to put them. Rashaun held Andria's hand, as they walked up to the door of the house. Rashaun released her hand briefly for him to unlock the door. He opened the door and came back to take her, taking her by the hand and led her into the house.

Once she entered the house, Andria immediately smelled the scented candles that permeated the air. The scent of fish was also in the air. He placed her bag on the off-white leather couch that they had recently purchased from Macys. "Baby, you did all this today?" Andria asked, looking around the room in amazement.

He brought her into their bedroom. There were flower petals on the bed, and two burning candles provided the soft light for the room.

"I feel like I'm in my own personal spa!" Andria exclaimed.

Rashaun helped her take her work clothes off, and she slipped into a short nightgown. As she reached for a panty to put on, Rashaun took her hand away from it.

"You definitely won't need this." He said, smiling.

"I won't, ah." She said.

"Let us go have dinner." Again, Rashaun took Andria's hand and walked downstairs with her.

Rashaun had dimmed the lights in the kitchen and led Andria to her seat.

Andria's head was woozy and her legs were tingling. She had never seen Rashaun act like this before. He had taken care of everything. She looked at him proudly. He was her man and she felt good saying that. She had never been treated like this in her entire life. They ate in silence, allowing their unspoken thoughts to fill the air.

"Rashaun, dinner was unbelievable." Andria said as they headed back up the stairs.

"I'm tired of words, I rather show you how much you mean to me." Rashaun said, as he kissed her lightly on the lips. Once inside the room, he removed her nightgown and looked at her. "You are beautiful."

He led her into the bathroom and the faint smell of the scented candles became much stronger. In the middle of the bathroom, there was a massage table.

"What is this?" Andria asked, as Rashaun took the oils off of the table. "You hired a masseuse?"

"Lie down on the table," he said softly.

"Okay." Andria said, feeling both nervous and excited at the same time.

Rashaun took the oil and rubbed it in his hands. He reached over and started to massage Andria, beginning with her fingers. He started with her fingers as he worked with his hands, moving smoothly but evenly all over her body. The energy in his fingers and body was more than any masseuse could give her. This was a labor of love. The time he spent in the massage class was paying off greatly now, with the "oh's and ah's" he was hearing coming from Andria. He could feel her body moving in a sexual flow now, letting herself go with each and every touch. His touching went as far as the inside of her legs, only an inch or two away from her vagina. She lifted her body for him to touch her there, but he resisted. Instead, he kept her purring more, as he teasingly massaged around her breasts, without touching her nipples. He moved his hands over her ears, and massaged the insides before he started working on her face, and then her head. By the time he was finished, Andria's vagina was dripping, and her body was feeling the most relaxed she had ever felt before. He gently nudged her off the table. Next, he took off his clothes and joined her in the whirlpool. There they relaxed for a few minutes, while he washed her down from head to toe. He then towel dried her and took her by the hand, leading her into the bedroom.

Once in the bedroom, he took a massager from the night stand and started to explore her body with it. Using his mouth along with the massager, he explored each and every sensuous point on her body.

"I didn't know you liked toys!" Andria gasped.

"I'm into your pleasure. If toys provide pleasure to you, I will work with it."

"Never used one before, but I guess we will be using it from now on." Andria said, as Rashaun moved the massager to her labia. He expertly moved it back and forth until Andria screamed, as her body shook in orgasmic glory.

Rashaun applied feathery touches to Andria's body with his fingers and tongue. He started with the extremities and brought it back to her stomach, and then finally, her vagina. He moved his tongue quickly, and as he did with the vibrator before, he started with her labia and worked his way back to her clitoris. His tongue flicked over the hood of her clitoris, going in a circular motion at first, then up and down and back and forth. It was at that point that her body began to shake again, uncontrollably this time. Once again he worked his way up her body, kissing her ears, her face, and her neck. He expertly flicked his tongue all over her, and provided suction at different points on her body. He waited for her body to yearn and beg for his entrance into her. At last he felt it, as her hips rose, begging for him to join her. He entered her slowly. He worked his way inside of her, letting her juices flow onto his manhood like a flooded stream. He moved with her, yet he controlled her movements, first starting with short thrusts, then long ones, as he built her up. He took her hand and put it over her clitoris, as she continued to rock back and forth. He found it to be a big turn on, and he encouraged her to play with her clitoris. She did, hesitantly at first, but as the pleasure built up, she worked her fingers vigorously over her clitoris, building up to a huge release. Once again her body convulsed with him, and it took all his self- control not to ejaculate and spoil the fun. It was then that he finally let her take control. She eagerly mounted him and started to work her vagina on his penis, squeezing him and letting him go. She rode him high and grinded on him low, and experienced orgasm after orgasm. She turned around and she worked him with her butt to his face, and he looked and enjoyed every part of her body. She called him names reserved for men that had committed evil deeds, and he called her words that he would never say to her otherwise. They made love and had sex until they couldn't do it anymore, and she fell asleep in his arms.

"You didn't come." She said to him.

"I didn't want to." He said. "I only wanted to enjoy your beauty. I wanted to feel and see you as I never did before."

"That you did."

"And I enjoyed every bit of it. I love the smell of you, I like the look of you, the taste, your moan, and your touch. I am truly blessed to have met you."

Andria looked at Rashaun, and in spite of all that transpired in her life, she knew that she had received a world of blessings. She felt his soul in her. The small light that was now burning in her was a testament to what their love was about. They had come together, and with God's help, they had created not once, but twice. Yes, this is the man that her life will forever be a part of. This is the man that she was going to live and die with.

Chapter XIV

*T*his is a big house." Lance said, as he followed Rashaun down the stairs.

"Yeah it's a far cry from the apartment. Now, my wife is driving me crazy with shopping for furniture and stuff for it." Rashaun picked up the remote and turned on the TV. "Every day she wants to buy something or do something."

"I like these leather couches," Lance said, as he sat down.

"They were the first things we bought."

"I had a designer consultant come in and change the look of our house recently. It cost us about a hundred grand by the time he was finished."

"Damn, I guess we got a bargain by using R&A designers."

"Who are they?"

"Rashaun and Andria."

"You are a fucking fool." Lance said, as he got comfortable on the couch. "It must be fun putting this whole place together."

Rashaun went into the refrigerator and took out two beers. "Yeah, it is sometimes, but after visiting the fifth store, I just want to come home and relax."

"It must be good to want to come home." Lance said, as he accepted the beer from Rashaun.

"Donald, you and your family were looking good at the dinner."

"You haven't called me that in years."

"It is your first name."

"Yeah, but I prefer to go by Lance. You know that. Donald reminds me of everything that is fucked up in my life. They say to be careful what you wish for, and I'm living proof of that."

Rashaun flipped the channel to MSNBC, "This black girl is hot."

Lance shrugged his shoulders and said, "They are all hot. I'm tired of all of them, the hot ones and the cold ones. My dick has been in so many pussies and mouths that I don't want shit right now. Sex without love is a waste of time. All it does is leave you depleted."

Rashaun looked over at his friend in disbelief. "Wait, the man that said all a woman could give him is her pussy and mouth, is now getting tired?"

"I have had threesomes, foursomes, did the group thing and whatever else is out there to be done, and I did it all. The end result is always the same thing, a shake and a roll. I really don't want to see another pussy anytime soon. Fucking for nothing is way overrated."

"I'm in shock here."

"Last night, my wife brought home this banging ass chick. They invited me in the room, but I didn't even go instead I went and slept in the guestroom."

"You know, you living the life that most men out there dream about. You know that?"

"Rashaun, you know that's not saying much. Right now, even with the abundance of pussy, some men are still jerking off."

Rashaun laughed. "You're right. But what happened? I thought you and your wife had come to an understanding. What changed?"

"It's the same shit over and over again, and I'm not getting anything from it. Sometimes when the woman is leaving, I wish my wife would leave with her, too. I want all of them to get the fuck out. My only joy right now is my son, Emerald. Do you want to hear a joke?"

"What's that?"

Lance shook his head. "Do you know that my wife wants us to have another child?"

"I don't see anything wrong with that."

"You don't see anything wrong with bringing a child into this environment? There is no love in our relationship. Our relationship is one of convenience."

"Does your wife know you feel this way?"

"Who gives a fuck whether she knows if I feel like that or not. I'm not leaving, and her ass ain't going, anyway." There was hopeless anger in Lance's voice.

Rashaun understood that his friend needed to vent. He didn't need advice, just an ear to listen to him. "I guess that means no."

Lance began to laugh. "You know you are right, most men would love to be in my position. You're living in one of the most expensive areas in Brooklyn. You drive a different luxury car, whenever you want. You have a wife that brings home a different woman for you and her. Or, sometimes you bring a woman home for you and your wife. You're even able to get up and leave anytime to go to an all- inclusive place in the Caribbean, and you have enough money to know that you can live the rest of your life like this. Dreams and fantasies do come true."

"Yes, they do."

"Then why the fuck am I dying to get out?" Lance slumped down into the chair.

"My friend, the answer lies within you."

"I envy you, you know that?"

"You envy me? I don't have half the shit that you have!"

Lance turned and looked at Rashaun. "But, you have the shit that matters. You have always been ahead of the game. You never let the game play you, you played the game, always knowing what you wanted the result to be. I think it was your mother that taught you that. I was never that lucky."

Rashaun tapped his friend on the shoulder. "I'm sorry."

"Sometimes I still wonder what life would be like with her. My grandmother told me that my mother was a good woman."

"I'm sure she was."

"I pursued the flash, while you went for the substance. I cannot tell you when the last time I held my wife and felt love for her. I'm sure you do that every day. My mother, my greatest love, had sent me down the worst path in life. I live a life without heart. But I'm not complaining, because it was also my choice."

"Are you okay?" Rashaun asked, showing concern in his voice for his friend.

"Am I okay? I doubt it, but I will survive." Lance gave a weak smile. "Yes, I will."

"Sometimes it's never too late to start over." Rashaun said.

Lance reached out and shook Rashaun's hands. "For me, it is. My life has been over for a long time."

"I don't think so, Lance. As long as you are breathing, your life is never over."

"Rashaun, you should reserve that comment for motivational speakers. You know as well as I do that some people are born losers, and others are born winners. There is nothing wrong with that, it is just the way life is."

"I believe people are what they make themselves out to be."

"Well, let's not get into a philosophical argument over it. I'm happy to see that you have bought a beautiful home. If you need any help, I'm available.'

"Lance, you can't even pound a nail into a piece of wood."

"Yeah you right, forget I offered that. I got to get out of here. I have a meeting in L.A. tomorrow morning, so I'm flying out tonight. What you getting into?" Lance asked opening the door.

"You never ask a man that has just bought a house a question like that. I have so much to do, that I don't even know where to begin."

"I forgot to ask you about the college girl. I think Brenda is her name."

Lance took his car keys out of his pocket. "Brenda isn't in college anymore. She is working for her father on Wall Street."

"You still with her?"

"Yeah, we do. I think I will ask her to head out to L.A. with me. She is good to hang with. We both know where we going with this. She likes my company, and I like hers, so we hang out together."

"Nothing in the wind?"

"Nah, nothing like that. I have been seeing Brenda for about four years, and I have never met any of her family members, and she hasn't met any of mine. Last year, she moved into this new apartment in Manhattan. I go and relax there sometimes. The last time I became close with someone, she left me and took all the money with her. I guess love is not meant for everyone. Anyway, got to go." Lance said, walking away.

"Later." Rashaun said.

Lance hit a button on his car's remote control and the doors rose up. He stepped into the car and the doors went down again. There was a thundering sound, as the black race car disappeared down the street.

Rashaun closed the door. He turned around and looked around the house. "Where the fuck do I start?"

Andria had her cell phone headset in her ear, as she drove to pick up Wisdom from her mother's house. She had accepted the fact that she would be Robin's listener, as she went through her sexual exploration.

"We went to a party last night!" Robin squealed over the phone.

"I hope you danced a lot." Andria said sarcastically, knowing full well that was not the kind of party Robin was talking about.

"I never knew that they held those things in apartment buildings. Greg's friend from work, the one we did it with, and thought we might like to check one out. When he told me the apartment, I was shocked."

"Where was it?" Andria inquired.

"Take one wild guess."

"At a church?"

"Andria, you are being ridiculous."

"Hey, that wouldn't surprise me."

"It was on the fifth floor of my building."

"Are you serious?"

"But, all those people in your building are professionals!" Andria exclaimed, the surprise evident in her voice.

"I know. The couple that hosted it was a doctor and a lawyer. All the people that came there were professionals. I have never seen so many lawyers, doctors, nurses and even executives in one room before."

Andria was trying to picture the couple that Robin was talking about. "We met them in the elevator once. A tall dark guy and a very light woman, with her hair pulled back in a ponytail."

"Yeah, that's her."

"But she looks…"

"Wake up Andria, innocence is for the children."

"I can't believe it."

"I didn't either, until I got there. Everyone was so well dressed, and there was even a bartender there. When I first got there, the music was playing and a few couples were dancing. I was sitting on the couch and this woman sat down next to me. I don't know what exactly happened, but the woman started to touch my hair and then my neck. I looked on the dance floor and a couple was kissing, and another person joined them, then they were all kissing. Before you know it, the girl had her tongue down my throat, and my husband had slipped her skirt off, and he was going down on her."

"These were all black people?"

"No. There were black, white Spanish and even Asian people there. My head got like totally crazy and I was all over the place. It was as if I was on drugs. This thing is totally intoxicating. I have never had so many orgasms in my life. At one point, I even saw Greg take a penis in his ass."

"Okay, Robin let's stop now. I think I've heard enough."

"But it was okay, we were just having fun. I don't think he is gay or anything. After it was over, everyone got dressed and it was like it never happened." Robin said. "I saw them in the elevator yesterday, and it was like we were just casual acquaintances once again."

Andria looked down at the phone and saw an unknown number blinking. "Robin, I have another call. We will talk later."

"Okay," Robin replied.

"Hello," Andria said, and spoke hesitantly into the phone.

"Hi, Andria." Kim said.

"Who is this?" Andria inquired.

"It is Kim."

"Kim, who? I don't know any Kim's."

"Your husband's ex-girlfriend."

"Where did you get my number?" Andria asked with shakiness in her voice.

Kim lay back on her sofa. "Where I got the number is not important. What I am about to tell you is."

"You just cannot leave us alone, can you?"

"I have already left you all alone. I have some news that I think is of great importance to you. I feel that if I was married, I would want to know this about my husband."

"Why do you think I will believe anything you have to say to me about Rashaun?"

"Andria, as you already know, I have been a lawyer for many years. I'm not going to give you any information without proof. I know I'm the last one you want to talk to, but I have to say I'm sorry and get this off my chest. George and I are about to get serious, but I feel I have to come clean with you before I can continue a relationship with him."

"I don't know why I'm even entertaining you, because my husband and I will not allow anyone to come between us. Our love is strong and true. I am telling you, whatever you have conjured up in your mind, will not work." Andria said, angrily.

Kim took her phone from her ear and pressed a few buttons. "Andria, I have just sent you a picture, did you receive it?"

"Yes, but I didn't look at it." Andria replied, nervously.

"Are you driving?"

"Yes."

"I would suggest that you pull over to the side of the road and look at that picture."

"Kim, who the hell do you think you are, ordering me to pull over to the side of the road? Whatever you have cannot affect me. Rashaun and I have been to the dumps with you and we still came out together, so I will look at your stupid picture, and then I want you to hang up the phone, and never call me again."

"Okay. I will give you your wish."

Andria quickly pulled up the picture on her cell phone. If this wasn't one of the bigger streets in Brooklyn, she would have ended up in someone's yard. But it was a big empty street, and she managed to swerve into the parking lane. Her hand trembled as she looked straight into Rashaun's eyes. Only it wasn't Rashaun she was looking at, it was a picture of Raqueen that Kim had sent her.

"Who is she?" Andria asked, turning off the car, as she slumped back in the car seat.

"She is my five year old daughter. And as you can see, her father is your husband."

"This is a mistake. You are lying. Rashaun hasn't been with you in over ten years. This is impossible."

"I thought you were going to say that, so we can prove it together." There was a dry, cold tone in Kim's voice. It was as though she was unaware of the effect her words were having on the woman on the other end of the line.

Andria was shaking. Her eyes had become swollen, and tears were about to burst out from them. It was as if she was being beaten mercilessly from an unknown source. She tried to say something into the phone, but no words came out.

"I understand this is a shock to you. Knowing that the man you thought was the love of your life, had gone out and done the unthinkable. But I don't want you to take my word for it. I will prove to you what you already know is true."

Kim took the remote and turned the TV on. Raqueen was at her grandparents, where Kim had left her since returning to New York.

"I will have to meet with you and your daughter."

"I know. Give me the time and the date."

"I will choose the company to run the test, but you will have to pay for it. Kim, if this turns out to be one of your diabolic games, someone will have to get your eyeballs out from under my fingernails."

"Girlfriend, I think you already know the answer to that. Raqueen is your husband's daughter, and he slept with me around the same time he impregnated you with Wisdom. I don't even want Rashaun anymore. After he had told me that you and he were not very serious. As you can tell, your husband is a rotten liar. I don't want that man anywhere close to me."

Andria wiped her eyes. She inhaled deeply, and her eyes became sharp and focused. She will go on with life as if nothing happened. "I will call you and give you the information on Monday."

"Okay. But can I give you a piece of advice?"

"No."

"If I were you, I wouldn't tell Rashaun about this conversation. He will want proof that all lawyers want, and that could lead to a lot of things. I don't want to have a fight with your husband, so I will keep this conversation between us."

Andria started the car. "I will do whatever I want to do. I told you, I don't want your advice."

"Talk to you later, girlfriend." Kim smiled, as she watched the reporters chasing the reality shore personality, "Snooki," on TV. "Everyone is a celebrity these days."

Andria again inhaled deeply, as she looked at the picture of Raqueen one more time. She had built a life around the man that she loved, and now it was all coming apart at the seams. She had made up her mind that she would fight anything that came between her and her husband, but now she was dealt a knockout blow, before she even began to fight. It took all of her resolve to pull back onto the road. The car was swerving a little, as if she was drunk. She was drunk all right, but not from alcohol. It was from emotions. She had decided that she wouldn't confront Rashaun with anything, and go on as if nothing ever happened. She lifted the phone and thought about calling Robin, but changed her mind and put the phone back down. This will have to be her fight. She could not go around talking about something that wasn't proven yet. What was she going to do if Raqueen was indeed Rashaun's child? It would mean that she was conceived at the pinnacle of their love. Rashaun had cheated on her, when the air they breathed seemed to involve only them. There was a rumbling in her stomach, but it wasn't from hunger. It reminded her that she was carrying a second child for a man who betrayed her.

She picked Wisdom up, and as soon as he saw the look on her face, she had to tell him that she wasn't feeling well. He offered to take care of her, but she told him that she would be alright. She just needed some rest. When she got home, she would go about her chores, as if nothing happened today. She would sleep with the enemy, without the enemy knowing that she had found out about him. It's been over five years since she had taken that vow, and only time and a test would prove whether she walks away or remains. She knew that if Raqueen was indeed Rashaun's child, she would never be able to love him again. She got home and made something for Wisdom to eat, and declined when he asked her to sit at the table and eat with him, as she always did. "No," she said, "I have to go and take a bath."

She went into the bathroom and turned on the shower. She quickly stepped into the shower, not even waiting for the cold water to become warm. She didn't feel the cold water running down her skin, mixing with the tears that were now escaping from her eyes. She didn't know how long she was in the shower before she felt his presence in the bathroom.

"Hi babes, you taking a long shower? Is everything okay?" Rashaun asked, as he took the toothbrush and began to brush his teeth.

"I'm okay," She managed to mumble, not turning the water, off just in case the tears started to fall again.

"Alright, I'm going to help Wisdom with his homework." Rashaun said, and he turned the faucet off.

She waited for him to leave the bathroom before stepping out of the shower. She took her time drying her skin, and looking at her face in the mirror. She didn't want him to see any remnants of the tears that overcame her while in the bathroom. Her eyes were puffy, but that could be attributed to her pregnancy. She slipped on a pair of slacks and a white T-shirt, before heading out of the room. She knew he would be waiting for her, so that they could eat together and talk about each other's day. This was one evening that she wouldn't be doing that. Any direct eye to eye contact right now would not be very wise. She needed to avoid him as much as possible. She walked out of the room, just as Wisdom was about to get up from the table.

"I'm going to give Wisdom a bath. Do you want to get dinner ready?" Rashaun asked, rising from the table with Wisdom.

"I will, but you men have to eat by yourselves this evening. I will warm up the leftovers."

"Are you okay? You know you have to eat a little more, because you are eating for two," Rashaun said.

"This is not my first pregnancy." She said, with anger and irritation in her voice.

"Okay, Honey, I was just trying to help." Rashaun said, taken aback by Andria's tone.

"We will be out in a few."

She didn't say anything else to him, feeling that the less she spoke to him, the better. There was turmoil going on inside of her right now, and she didn't know how to control it. She reached into the refrigerator and took out the leftover lasagna. She had baked it in a large pan, and was actually surprised by how good it came out. Last night, she had two servings of it. Rashaun and Wisdom looked at her as if she was trying to win a fast food eating contest. Now, the food did nothing for her appetite. Andria heated the food up in the microwave, and put it on the table for Rashaun and Wisdom. She walked over to the living room and turned on the TV. She sat down on the couch to watch the TV. It was tuned to "Noggin," a favorite channel of Wisdom's. She didn't change the channel. Instead, she looked right through the television, as Rashaun and Wisdom sat down to eat.

Thirty minutes later, Rashaun put Wisdom in his bed and then joined Andria on the couch. She didn't even look at him, as he sat down and put his arm around her. She continued to stare straight ahead, and moaned, as if her stomach was hurting her. He change the channel to MSNBC, and sat back to watch the news. Andria waited a few minutes, and then she got up.

"You tired?" he asked.

"Yeah, and I don't feel so good." She said, as she rubbed her stomach. "I think I will turn in for the night."

"I will stay out here for a while and catch up on the news, unless you want me to come in and rub your stomach." Rashaun said, turning around to look at Andria.

"No, that's fine. We will talk tomorrow." Andria said, and turned and walked into the bedroom.

Once in the bedroom, Andria lay down on the bed. Her mind went back to the first time she met Rashaun at the club, all the way to the shootout in the church, and the birth of Wisdom. They had gone through some good times and some hard times, but love was always on their side. Trust and honesty were the bedrocks of their relationship. She sometimes didn't know if she would wake up tomorrow, but she knew that if she did, Rashaun's love for her would always be there. She turned the light off, just in case he came in and noticed that she wasn't asleep. She really didn't want to chit chat with him tonight. She was hoping to fall asleep before he came in and put his hands around her, as he always did. It was the hands that she longed for on so many nights. The hand that made her feel secure, and sent the waves of his love all throughout her body. No, she didn't want him touching her now. She would feel dirty, betrayed and even scorned. He had lived with her with a lie so monumental, that for the rest of their lives, it would always be present. A child is not a video, a word, a thought, or an action. A child is a living thing. Whenever you see the child, you are reminded that the life you are living is a lie.

Rashaun came into the room about forty five minutes later, but her eyes were not heavy and sleep was far away. He didn't know she was sleeping, so he wrapped his hands around her. She pushed him away, because she couldn't do it.

"I'm sorry Baby, but my stomach doesn't feel so good," she said to him.

"Should I call the doctor?" He asked, concerned.

"No, the doctor already told me that there would be nights like these. It is all part of the pregnancy."

"What do you want me to do?" He asked, concerned.

"You don't have to do anything. Just go to sleep. I think I will call in sick, tomorrow." She replied, hating to lie to him, but doing it out of necessity.

'Okay, if I fall asleep and you need me, please wake me up." He reached over and kissed her on the cheek.

"I will." She said, and went back to staring into the darkness of the room.

Rashaun was asleep in ten minutes.

Andria would go without sleep for the night.

Chapter XV

*H*e didn't know why he was there, but there he was. In the midst of it all, there were people singing and children snickering. He used to go to these things when he was a little boy. When he was growing up, his parents made sure he attended every Sunday. Paul and him were the two trouble makers in the neighborhood. This time, it was him alone, because Paul was now buried in a cemetery on Cortelyou Road. Tears welled up in his eyes, as he thought about his brother. They had been inseparable as teenagers, until Paul left for the States. As did so many West Indian parents, they believed that America held the key to advancement and prosperity. His parents made a big deal about it, too. They threw a big party before Paul left, and at Sunday service, the Pastor mentioned that Paul was leaving for the U.S. The Pastor wished Paul the best, and he asked the small congregation to pray for him as he went abroad. That was a long time ago.

His parents had come to the United States to bury their son, but he didn't have a visa. He looked at his parents before they boarded the plane for the states. They looked broken hearted and weak. His mother had told him that she never thought that she would be going to the U.S. to bury her son, but here she was. They had discussed bringing him back to Jamaica for the burial, but they knew that Paul would have wanted to remain in the U.S. His mother had spoken to him about this girl that Paul was living with at one time, a woman he said he was planning to marry. She was going to have his kids and eventually, he and his wife and kids, would come to Jamaica to visit them. Later on, his mother found out that Paul had broken up with her. He never even knew the name of the woman. If he did, he would have found her in the U.S., and tell her that his brother was planning to marry her before he died. That was water under the crumbling bridge now, and soon the bridge wouldn't even exist anymore.

Fish wiped the tears from his eyes, and acknowledged the woman that had seen him in his time of weakness.

"God bless you. Put your faith in Him," she said. The woman wore a bright pink and black dress, and had her hands wrapped around her two young boys.

The time for putting his faith in God had passed. God had forsaken him and his brother. What he had to do now, rested in his own hands. He got up off the chair and turned his body around, squeezing himself out of the pew. All eyes were on him as he walked out of the church during the middle of the service, but he didn't care. He had things to do. The airline ticket in his pocket had a lift off date a week from now. He watched Rashaun's movements for the past two weeks, and knew that Wednesday was his late night. That's when he planned to pick him up and take him to the garage. He had already laid the plastic bags down in the garage to use after he dismembered the body, and would use them to take it out in pieces. He was going to cut him up, as he did for so many of the American tourists, when they came to the fish yard and wanted their fish cleaned. He'd gut the fish and cut them into small pieces. Suddenly, he felt his phone vibrating, and quickly pulled it out of his pocket. It was an 876 number, the area code for Jamaica.

"Wah up girl?" He said, reverting back to his Jamaican dialect.

"Mi miss you bad." His girl on the receiving end replied.

"I see you using all of the Digital 1200 Minutes calling plan." He said, with a smile coming over his face.

"Yeah, me pay the money. And me like talking to you bad." She said.

"Me love talking to you, too."

"What you cooking tonight?"

"I'm going to cook some fried breadfruit and fry some fish. I went down there yesterday to check on the boat, and Talbott gave me a bunch of fish."

"Talbott is a good guy."

"He asked me when you coming back, and I told him in a week."

"He said he hopes so, because his sister went to the United States on vacation once, and never returned."

"You coming back eh, Fish?" her voice was now trembling a little.

"Girl, me told you, I am mi got ma ticket in ma bag, now. Jamaica is where my life is."

"Me thing miss you bad, too."

"Last night, mi was so horny."

"Me too. I can't wait to get me some of your pork."

"Well, you better be ready when you come home, because I'm going to ride you day and night."

"Me look forward to it. You seen my parents?"

"Yeah, me go by and visit them on Sunday. They doing good. I told them that you coming home next week, so they excited to see you coming back. They don't want you to stay in America at all."

"I know."

"I think it's because they got bad feelings from what happened to

Paul. I told them don't worry, you not staying. Did you buy those shoes for me?"

"Yeah, I go to the store with the clipping you sent me from the internet, and I got all five colors." Fish didn't tell her that he also bought three more pairs of shoes that were recommended by this Jamaican girl he had met in the store. She said his wife going to love it bad.

"I also bought the dresses and skirts, too. You know, everything is cheaper in the U.S."

"I'm going to really have to put it on you, when you get home." Mindi said.

"Yeah, but just take it easy, might not have all the strength after been eating all this rich American food."

"But I heard America got all the food you find in Jamaica."

"Yeah, they got it, but it's not the same."

"Well me gonna get you fat when you come home. My break is over, and I got to get back to work."

"Me love you. I'm going to call you tonight."

"Me love you, too. Will talk later." Fish said, hanging up the phone. Mindi would think he was mad if he told her that he had just come from church. She knew that he didn't like going to church, and had stopped attending a long time ago. He had already sent out two barrels to Jamaica, filled with all the purchases he made. He had found a place in the city where he could get fishing equipment below cost. He had purchased a lot of it, so he could sell to the guys by the bay. Yesterday, he had gone to his cousin's house and told them that he was leaving in a week. He had to tell them that he couldn't take much of their stuff back to Jamaica, because the airlines were only allowing one piece of luggage now, and they would have to pay to have him to take another piece. They said they would ship it in a barrel, because it would be cheaper. He concurred with them.

Again, Fish's phone started to vibrate. He looked down at the screen. As expected, it was Jessica. The cell phone was his only means of communicating with Jessica, because he didn't have a phone in the apartment. As he walked to the train station, he thought about what little Jessica really knew about him. Presently, she only knew that he lived in Jamaica, but didn't know exactly where. She didn't even know his first or his last name. She didn't know where his cousins lived. If he disappeared today, she wouldn't know where to find him.

George knew exactly where to find Rashaun, and as he walked up the stairs to Rashaun's office, he felt very nervous. He didn't know what he was going to say to his friend of twenty years, but he knew that he had to have this conversation. He had been unable to reach Rashaun since the dinner party. Rashaun refused to answer his phone when he called, and didn't return his messages. George had never been in such a predicament before, because friendship was a choice thing. Someone either wanted to be your friend, or they didn't. But he and Rashaun were more brothers than friends, and he didn't want to give up his brother.

George knocked on his friend's office door. He knew Rashaun wouldn't just open the door, he would get closer to it. In New York City, you can't just open the door when you are not expecting someone. George was hoping he would still open it, once he knew that it was him at the door.

"Who is it?" Rashaun's voice came powerfully through the door. That was another thing about answering doors. In the city, you should never sound as though you were a little wimp behind the door.

"It's George, can I talk to you?"

There was a hesitation at first. George counted at least thirty seconds that had gone by before the door finally opened. He stepped into the door, but Rashaun was nowhere in sight. George quietly closed the door behind him, and walked through the waiting room and into Rashaun's office. Rashaun was standing behind his desk, looking out the window.

"How you been, Rashaun? I have been trying to call you, but you don't pick up my calls."

"George, let's not beat around the bush. After over twenty years of friendship, you walked into my house, with a woman that you knew had brought me great pain and suffering. It was like walking into a room with a gun, and shooting me and my family."

"That was not my intention, Rashaun, and you should know that."

"Then, what the fuck was it?" Rashaun said, angrily. "Not in a hundred years, did I see that coming from you."

"Sometimes things happen in life that is beyond one's control."

"That's fucking bullshit."

"You didn't just happen on Kim. Poison is all around us, but we don't just get it in our mouth, someone has to put it there. Who put Kim in your mouth?"

George looked over at his friend, whose anger was boiling over right now. "What can I say, I fell in love."

Rashaun laughed a slow deliberate laugh. "You fell in love? You are not fucking serious."

George sat down on the chair and leaned back. "I didn't come here to fight with you. I didn't come here to justify what I did. Kim and I are two adults, with the freedom to date whomever we want. I came here, because I value our friendship."

Rashaun shook his head. "You value our friendship?"

"Are you still in love with Kim? Because as someone on the outside looking in, it looks like you do." George said.

"George, any feelings I had for Kim died a long time ago. Now, if you ask me if I feel sorry for that witch, I will say yes. For someone to go around trying to destroy someone and is willing to do anything to accomplish that, is very sad."

"Are you upset that I'm dating Kim? Did I break some kind of manly code or something?"

"Now you are getting beside yourself. I really do not care who Kim dates, whether it's you, or a bum on the street. If you came to me and told me that you were dating Kim, I would have given you one piece of advice, and that would be for you to watch your back."

George straightened himself up in the chair. "We used to talk a lot about Kim, but she is not the person that you think she is. Maybe years ago she was like that, but she ain't like that anymore."

Rashaun sat down on the chair behind his desk. "George, you remember that woman who lived down the block from me, and she used to fuck around on her husband?"

"Yeah."

"You remember what you used to say about him?"

"Yeah, I used to say, that his head was so far up his ass, that he was blinded by ass," George responded.

"Well George, you have become that man."

"You know what, Rashaun? I came here this afternoon to set things right, because I should have told you about me and Kim, before I brought her to your house. I admit that I fucked up there. But now, you are insulting me. So you know what, fuck you! I don't need you, and neither does my woman!"

Rashaun turned his back. "Goodbye, George. I will be praying for you, because you have fallen for the black widow."

"Don't worry about me Rashaun, worry about yourself." George pulled the door shut.

Rashaun sat back in his chair and looked out the window. A friend of over twenty years was no more.

Andria's eyes were sleepy, and her fingers were trembling. She wondered what affect her stressful condition was having on the baby growing inside her. On the opposite of her, Kim sat, as composed and relaxed as ever. Andria hated her with every bone in her body. Kim had insisted that she be there when the results came back, because she wanted to make sure that Andria heard the truth. No matter what the result, Andria wanted to make sure that Kim didn't see her in tears. She had to be strong. She had to rise above this, not only for her, but for Wisdom and the child she now carried.

The receptionist had her hair up in a pig tail, and appeared to be a young girl of no more than twenty years old. She pulled the separation glass back. "The doctor will see you guys now. Please go through the door on your right," she said, before pulling the glass back closed, and delved back into her book.

Andria gingerly got up from the chair and followed Kim, who walked gracefully into the office, holding the door open for Andria to follow.

"Have a seat, ladies." The male doctor looked young, and hadn't even greyed yet.

"I don't know your situation, but before I give you the results, I want you both to know that there is counseling available for both of you. Do either of you want to take advantage of the counseling since the first two sessions are free?" The doctor asked, looking at both of them.

Andria and Kim both shook their heads in unison.

"Oh, and I have to mention one last thing. You both are aware of the reality shows and the talk shows out now? I have to ask both of you a question, would either of you want to participate in the Lipton reality show? Both of you will receive two thousand dollars each, if you agree to do it."

Kim looked at him as though he was crazy. "No, thank you doctor, now can we get to the results?"

"Well, the test was positive. There was a positive match for both the father and the child."

"No!" Andria yelled out, and she began sobbing.

Kim reached over to the doctor and shook his hand. "Thank you, doctor."

"Everything was a lie!" Andria's body shook from the sobs.

Kim walked over to Andria and hovered over her for a minute. "No one is perfect." She said, and walked out the door.

The doctor came over and pulled his chair up next to Andria. "Is there anything I can do for you?"

"No. Just give me ten minutes, and I will leave."

"I don't think you should be driving in this condition. Do you want me to call a cab?"

"I took the bus here," she said. "I will call a friend to pick me up."

"Don't you want me to call your husband?" the doctor asked, looking at her wedding ring.

"No, I'm fine." Andria said. "Just give me some time to get myself together."

"Okay, take your time. I will be right here if you need me." The doctor went and sat back in his chair and picked up the phone and dialed a number.

Andria pulled her phone out of her bag. She pressed down heavily on the phone, speaking briefly into it. "My friend will be here in fifteen minutes. I will go outside and wait for her shortly."

"Take your time." The doctor said, covering his phone with his hand.

Andria wanted to get up and walk away right now, but her legs were too weak to move so she remained seated, because she was afraid of falling. She was lucky that Robin was living downtown Brooklyn, which wasn't very far from where she was on Boerum Street. Andria didn't tell her anything about what was going on with her. She only asked her to come and get her right now. Robin asked her if she was okay, but all Andria would tell her was to hurry. Andria sat back in the chair and wished she wasn't born.

By the time Andria sat in Robin's car, the remnants of dried up tears were clearly visible on her cheeks.

"What are you going to do?" Robin asked, with a measure of concern in her voice.

"I will do the only thing I can do. I will move in with my mother." Andria said, her voice passive, but strong.

"What about Wisdom?"

"I will never prevent Rashaun from seeing his child, but I'm sure he will have to divide his time now. He does have a daughter, also." Andria didn't know why she said that, but it seemed like she needed to.

"I don't think Rashaun will love Wisdom any less now." Robin said.

Andria looked out the window past the cars and trees, and up into the beautiful blue skies. "I don't know the man I married, the one I lay down with night after night."

"Tell me about it."

"When I get home, I will tell him what happened today, and then I will take Wisdom and my stuff and walk out." There was dryness in Andria's voice.

"It seems we used to have such happier times."

"If I didn't have this child in my womb, I would go out and drink until the sky falls to the earth."

"Girl, that is not all that it's cracked up to be. A few days ago, I got home, Greg and his friend from work were fucking in my bed. They both asked me if I wanted to join them. I knew it was over, then. I have been going to bed drunk since."

Andria looked back at all the packages in the back seat. "That's why you went on a shopping spree."

"I thought that if the alcohol didn't help me, maybe spending money would."

"I'm sorry, Robin, I was so caught up with my life that I forgot to ask you how you are doing."

"Believe me, Andria, your issues are much larger than mine. My husband already confessed to me that he is gay, and he thanks me for bringing it out in him. He told me that he would never have realized it, otherwise. I think he wanted to give me a medal."

"What?"

Robin laughed. "And, get this. He doesn't think the marriage has to be over. Can you believe it? He still wants us to stay married."

Andria seemed to momentarily forget about her own situation. "What did you tell him?"

"I told him, Honey, I do understand we are living in modern times, and there are lots of couples out there that are living like this, but I'm not going to be one of them. Now, take your things and move them into the guest room until you could get the fuck out."

"What about my Godchild?"

"I told him to go and talk to your daughter, because you don't want me to do it. She is in High School now, and she would understand."

Andria looked puzzled. "Are you sure that he wasn't seeing his co-worker for the whole time?"

Robin looked at her friend and smiled. "I thought the same thing, and even I asked him about it."

"What did he say?"

"He swore up and down that he didn't."

"Do you believe him?"

"Let's say, I had this girlfriend once that swore up and down that she had never touched a woman sexually. She claimed that if any woman would try to go down there, she would have to kill them. Do you know what happened?"

"You learned that she used to service all the women in the WNBA?"

"That's good, but that's not it. I found out that while she was saying all that, she was practically living with a woman. But enough about me, my relationship had been over for a long time and I just didn't want to accept it."

"Maybe you guys might still be able to work it out."

"For me to do that, I would have to grow a big fat dick, because that's what his man's got. And that's not happening. But you and Rashaun, that's another story."

"Robin, what the hell happened to our lives? A year ago, everything was going great."

"Was it? Maybe we closed our eyes to the cracks in the glass, and eventually it got so big, that it shattered."

"Well, at least Paula's relationship is going good. And who would have guessed that, with that old man of hers."

Robin and Andria laughed for the first time. It was a laughter not denoting happiness, but a release of all the tension and frustration that was plaguing their lives.

"Rashaun is a bastard. The other night, that man put some loving on me that I'm still trying to recover from."

"And today, he ripped your heart out."

"That's a man for you." Andria concluded, her eyes once more clouded over with pain. "But women are even worse."

"Yeah, I know what you mean. That woman Kim ain't no joke."

Andria cringed with pain when she thought about Kim and the way she sat, feeling so confident that the test would prove that Rashaun was the father of her child. "Yeah, you should have seen her sitting there, almost laughing at my torment."

Robin tapped her friend on the shoulder. "Sometimes in life, what goes around, comes around. She will get hers someday."

"You know what? Maybe I shouldn't say anything to Rashaun. I should just go ahead with my life as if nothing happened," Andria said.

"That will blow Kim's mind, Andria, if you could do that, it would send Kim to the crazy house."

"Yeah, it would, wouldn't it?" Andria smiled.

"By the way, how did you get the blood from Rashaun for the DNA test?" Robin asked.

"It was pure luck. Rashaun hates blood. He was trying to take out a piece of glass from one of the picture frames, and he cut himself. Of course, the first thing he did was call me. I had a first aid kit, and when he turned his face, I let some of the blood drip into a small cup."

"Andria, you are devious."

"Sometimes, you got to do what you got to do."

Chapter XVI

*G*eorge had done what he thought he had to do. However, the results of his actions did not sit well with him. As he walked over to Kim's apartment building, he knew for certain that he had ended a friendship that went back more than a score. Rashaun didn't give him a choice, and now he knew that he would never speak to him again.

"What's up George?" The doorman, who was middle aged, reached out and shook his hand.

"Not much, Sal. How is the family?" George asked. As was his nature, George made friends easily, and had gotten to know Sal. Sal's wife was home recovering from a hip operation, and he also had a thirty-year old son, who was a victim of the recession.

"Good today, but hoping that tomorrow will be better," Sal said. I will notify her that you're coming up."

"Thanks, Sal. Keep up that good spirit," George said, as he headed towards the elevator.

The door to Kim's apartment was open when he got upstairs, and he walked right in. Kim was talking on her cell phone, so he went into the refrigerator and took out a beer. He opened it, and sat down in front the couch.

"Let me guess, it didn't go well with Rashaun," Kim said, joining him on the couch.

"Sometimes this boy refuses to listen. I went to him to apologize, thinking that we could work it out. He wouldn't listen to a word I had to say. He only spoke about his hatred towards you."

"Me?"

"Yeah. He thinks you are using me, to get to him."

"That damn boy has gone and lost his cotton picking mind. I'm not even thinking about Rashaun."

"I told him so. But his mind is set on this, and nothing else. He doesn't understand that I love you, and that we are building something here."

Kim reached out with her right hand, to turn George's cheek towards her. "George, you just said that you loved me."

"Does that surprise you?"

"I don't know what to say. I wasn't expecting that."

George took a major gulp of his beer.

Kim moved onto George and sat on his lap, with her face directly in front of him. She kissed him gently on the lips.

"There you go, starting up again." George said, and reached out and kissed her solidly on the lips.

"Me? Innocent me, starting something?" She said, as she reached out to kiss George above the eyes and continued kissing him all over his face.

"You are so fucking dangerous." He moaned, feeling his manhood rise.

"What are you going to do about it?" Kim said, running her hands over George's stiff dick.

"The only thing a man in this situation would do." George said, lifting Kim's shirt above her head.

"You don't waste any time, do you?" Kim said, as she felt George's lips on her tits. She pulled the short skirt she was wearing up over her thighs and unbuttoned George's pants, to free his manhood.

"You are naughty." He said, as he adjusted himself so that Kim could have access to him.

"You want me?" She asked, running her hands over his chest.

"Yes, I do. I want you bad." He groaned, while the tip of his penis brushed against Kim's pubic hairs.

"How much do you want me?" Kim teased, while brushing her pubic hair over his erect penis.

"Every minute, every hour, whether I'm awake, or dreaming. I want you always." He now began sucking hard on her breasts.

"Are you sure that you want me?"

"Yes baby, I do."

"Then you can have me." With that, she clamped her vagina onto his erect penis. Her wetness made it easier for him to access her womanhood. She began to ride him softly and slowly at first, as he worked on her breasts. Her tongue flicked in and out of his ears, and her hands raced along his back. Their mouths hungrily found each other, as their bodies continued to move in and out. The buildup started in her body and continued to grow, as she worked her waist back and forth. He levitated off the couch, reaching out to her, as he watched her eyes begin to flutter. Her vagina began to contract tightly on his penis, as the root of her orgasm floated up, taking over her body. As she moved with him, she loved the feeling of taking him, in and then slowly letting him go. Her pace became faster now and he noticed the intense look of pleasure in her face. He looked into her dreamy eyes, and her heart beat faster, as her body began to shake and slowly start to jerk. She lay on top of him now, with his penis still erect inside of her. Her body made three more slow jerks, and she buried her head in his neck. Her hair brushed against him, ever so lightly. Slowly, she lifted herself off of him, and traced her hands down his chest, raking his chest with her nails. She eased herself onto the floor, so that she was now kneeling in front of him, with her hands on his dick. Then, she rose back up and sucked hard on his nipples, and he moaned as she bit them, ever so gently. She felt his penis throbbing in her hand. She made her way down to his navel, flicking in and out, then circling the head of his penis, she continued her downward decent. Her mouth was now going around his balls, licking and sucking, while she pulled gently on his penis. Next, she ran her tongue from the base of his penis, all the way up the sides. At the top, she created a vacuum with her mouth, and sucked on him, ever so gently.

"What the…" he gasped, and before he could complete the sentence, she had engulfed his entire manhood into her mouth.

He lost control now, and exploded in her mouth, sending the potential birth of a million George's scurrying down her throat.

"Fuck!" George moaned, as he held her head over his dick, letting her suck him dry. When she finally lifted her head from his penis, he saw the face of an angel, an angel that was his to love.

◎◎◎

The woman who was now looking at Rashaun did not have the face of an angel. She would more aptly be described as the reincarnation of the devil. His wife's eyes sent daggers of fire throughout his body, over and over again.

"Yes, Rashaun, DNA don't lie!" Andria yelled, pushing the paper in front of him.

"Raqueen *is* your daughter!"

"And you learned that from?" Rashaun was angry, but he tried not to show it.

"Your girlfriend, Kim."

Rashaun rolled his eyes, but his voice was steady as he spoke. "Kim gave you this piece of paper and you believed her?"

"No Rashaun, I'm not stupid. I went with Kim to a doctor of my choosing."

"You went to the doctor with Kim with my DNA and her daughter's DNA, to prove that I was the child's father. And, you did all that without my consent or knowledge."

"Yes Rashaun, and please don't go there. Please don't try to shift the conversation from the weapon, to the murder. It doesn't matter how I found out that Raqueen is your daughter. The point remains the same. Kim told me that she fucked you around the same time that you were sleeping with me. I can't even argue with her, with proof like that."

Her voice was now calm and in control of her emotions, even though she was raging with inner turmoil.

"Well, how can I argue with proof that is 99.6 % accurate? All I can do is to tell you that I didn't sleep with Kim, and if the child is mine, it must have occurred by some miracle."

"That's it? That's all you going to say? I didn't do it!"

"Yes, that's all I'm going to say. What I will do, is prove to you that I didn't sleep with Kim. I don't know how I'm going to do this, but I will. I have never been unfaithful to you, from the time we started seeing each other, and I don't think I ever will. Now if you want to believe that I had an affair with a woman, who by all her actions, is obviously trying to destroy my family, then go ahead."

"I'm moving in with my mother for the next few days," Andria said.

"There is no need for that. I am leaving. I won't be back until I can prove to you that I didn't have an affair with Kim. If that is the only way to have a child with someone, then the child is definitely not mine." Rashaun went into the bedroom and took his briefcase. 'I'm going to give Wisdom a kiss good night."

Andria watched Rashaun walk into the room, and come back out a few seconds later.

"Why?" Andria asked, with tears streaming down her cheeks.

"I know you have the card to our account, but if you need additional money, here is my credit card, and it has an unlimited balance. You can buy whatever you want, I don't care. If you don't mind, I will pick up Wisdom from school and talk to him tomorrow." Rashaun walked towards the door. "And as I said before, I have never been unfaithful to you."

Rashaun opened the door and walked out.

Andria stood in the same spot she had been standing in throughout the whole conversation. It was as if she was stuck there.   She didn't expect him to respond the way he did. He was stoic in his response, and she really didn't understand it. He didn't deny that the child was his, yet he denied having an affair with Kim. How can you have a child with someone else and not sleep with her? Rashaun had never donated his sperm to a sperm bank, did he? Slowly she moved her right foot, then her left, and was able to walk to the chair in the kitchen. She sat down and held her head in her hands. She lifted her head up and placed her right hand on her stomach, and slowly began to rub it for comfort.

"Little girl, I don't know what world I'm bringing you into," she sighed, looking down at her stomach.

Rashaun held his head high, as he walked down the steps of his house. He turned back, and looked at the house one more time, before he began his walk down the street. It was in the dead of night, and he swung his briefcase at his side, not knowing where he was going. He thought about how the impossible could now become possible. Even though he knew he hadn't slept with Kim, he wondered, as he thought back, that maybe he was intoxicated at some point, and had no recollection if he had been with her or not. None of the memories he had of her, included this ever happening. He unlocked his phone, passed over George's name in the "favorite" section of his cell phone address book.

"Yeah, can you meet me at the diner?" He spoke into the phone. "It doesn't matter what time. I have all night."

Rashaun put the phone back into his pocket and headed towards the neon light that advertised "Sunset Diner" which was open 24 hours a day. In the diner, he sat behind a group of six young black men and women. Each of them had a large plate of food in front of them. He remembered those days, eating like mad, before going out all night to dance his heart out. Rashaun ordered a cup of tea from a waitress who seemed as though she had enough of the young people, as she rolled her eyes, as they became more boisterous. Rashaun sipped the tea slowly. He was now a man without a home. He was a husband without a wife, a father without his child. It was a lonely and painful feeling, and he did everything that he could, to keep his emotions in check. He didn't want to be in a diner in the middle of the night. He wanted to be home, curled up in bed next to his wife, rubbing her stomach.

He saw Lance walking into the diner, looking lean and fit. He arrived an hour after Rashaun did, and was now taking a complete visual tour of the place.

"You acting like a cop." Rashaun said to Lance, as he pulled a chair out from the table.

"I know, the business I'm in makes me that way. I got to see everything that's around me at all times." Lance said, sitting down on the chair. "What the fuck did you do to Andria that she has you sitting in a diner in the middle of the night?"

"I left the house." Rashaun answered.

"You left the house! Why the fuck would you do that?"

"It was either I leave, or she was going to leave."

"What the hell happened?"

"I'm the father of Kim's child." Rashaun replied.

"Are you sure? I was only kidding when I asked you about that." Lance asked.

"Nope, I'm not kidding. She had the proof there in a DNA sample. They say that DNA is almost a hundred percent accurate. I knew then, that I couldn't argue the fact that I wasn't the father."

"Yeah, I know that. I had a DNA test done when my son was born, because I know the game, and the game is dirty." Lance continued. "You slipped up?"

"No. I never slept with Kim. The last time I slept with Kim was in college, so unless she froze my sperm, it didn't happen." Rashaun said.

"I had to punch this fucking chick once, to get my sperm out of her mouth. She wanted to have my baby. Her teeth and my sperm splattered all over the place. It cost me ten grand, but I didn't mind. But, how the hell did Kim get pregnant with your child, if you never slept with her?" Lance asked.

"It's my marriage question."

"Did you ever donate your sperm or anything like that?" Lance looked puzzled.

"Lance, it's me you talking to."

"Yeah, I realize that now, so forget I asked that."

"Been going over it in my head, but can't seem to come up with any answers."

Lance reaching. " You know, women sometimes obtain fake DNA results. With a computer and a printer and modern technology, you can do almost anything these days."

"No, Andria chose the doctor, and even went with her to take the test." Rashaun commented.

"You knew about it?"

"No."

"Then how did Andria get your…"

"I don't know. She said, that's not important right now and I agree wither.. I will deal with her on that and other issues later. Right now, I want to know how the fuck I had a child, when I didn't even sleep with the child's mother."

"That's a tough one."

"And I'm stranded now, without any transportation. I left the truck with Andria, in case she needed it to get around."

Lance put his finger out to stop Rashaun from talking. "Hold on," he said. Lance pulled out his phone and made a call, speaking briefly into it.

"What's that about?" Rashaun asked.

"Don't worry about it. Have you considered how you are going to prove that you didn't sleep with Kim? Because you cannot prove that the child isn't yours, since no one goes up against DNA evidence."

"Yeah, I know."

"Well, if you did not put the cake in the oven, then someone else had to have put it there. If you can, find the person that put the cake in the oven, then maybe how they got the ingredients wouldn't be important."

"Kim was pregnant while she lived in Washington, and that's where she had the baby. She won't give me that information. I'm so worried, because I just bought the house, and you know, money is tight right now."

"That's why you have friends. I know this private investigator that helped me find my father. That man could find a gray hair in the cracks of an elephant's ass."

"I can't afford him."

"Don't worry about it," Lance said.

"Thanks." Rashaun said, as he watched a very large black man wearing a track suit, walk into the diner. Rashaun watched the man as he walked over to their table.

"What's up?" Lance said, seeing the petrified look on Rashaun's face.

Rashaun raised his head in the direction of the big man, who was now rapidly approaching.

Lance turned around to look, and stood up as the man approached their table. The man placed a set of keys into Lance's hand, stepped back, and stood by the door.

"You know him?" Rashaun asked.

"Yeah, he used to work for my stepfather, and now he works for me. I think he is a little pissed that I got him out of bed."

"I wouldn't like that man getting pissed at me. That's one big motherfucker."

Lance dismissed Rashaun's concern with a wave of his hand. "Hurricane is a gentle giant. Now, here are the keys to the X6 that is outside. All the paperwork is in the car. Use it as long as you want."

"What? I can't take that!"

"I don't think Hurricane would let you take it. It was given to you. Now, do you need a place to sleep tonight?"

"Nah, I'm going to head over to my father's place."

"Anyway, I got to go and drop Hurricane back at his house. I will have the investigator get on this tomorrow, so don't worry about it. You will be back at home before you know it."

"Thanks man, I owe you one." Rashaun said, giving Lance a bear hug.

"Don't worry about it. We take care of our own." Lance said, and turned around and walked away.

Rashaun paid the waitress, then got up and walked to the truck, realizing that tomorrow was his long day at work, and he needed to get some rest so that he could think clearly.

Chapter XVII

*I*t was 9:30 p.m. by the time Fish saw Rashaun locking up the office. Fish was standing in the entranceway of an abandoned building, one that was slated to be demolished and rebuilt. Rashaun carried his briefcase in his hand, as he walked towards the car. Fish had been looking at Rashaun from different areas of the block, including the coffee shop and the paint store, that were located across the street. All of the stores were closed now, with the coffee shop being the last one to shut down for the night. Rashaun usually looked around before he closed up the office, but he didn't do that tonight, which meant that he had something on his mind. Fish also noticed that Rashaun was driving a different car tonight, not the green Mercedes Benz truck that he usually drove. He waited patiently for Rashaun to pass, hiding further in the shadows of the building. His nerves were on end, but he knew it had to be done tonight, or else it would never happen. He needed to do what he had to do, and then in two days, he would be back home in Jamaica.

Rashaun was feeling very tired, since he hadn't slept at all last night. He was now without his family, and between that, and having to hear a lecture from his father, he found it difficult to sleep. He did not tell his father exactly what happened, except for the fact that he had a fight with Andria, and he needed someplace to stay for a few days. His father lived in a two bedroom apartment, and the second bedroom was made into a bedroom for Wisdom, filled with toys and funny shapes painted on the walls. Rashaun slept in that room. Rashaun felt useless, while waiting for the private investigator that Lance had hired, get back to him. Lance had called him and told him that he would have something by the weekend. Earlier on in the day, Rashaun had picked up Wisdom from school, and dropped him home to Andria. He didn't go up to the door. Instead, he waited by the car, while his son went inside.

"Keep walking." Fish commanded, as he buried the gun in Rashaun's side.

"What?" Rashaun didn't know where the man had come from.

"Open the car and get in!" Fish shouted, as they approached the BMW.

"What car?"

Fish slammed the gun into Rashaun ribs. "Don't fuck with me!"

Rashaun pressed the remote and opened the car door. He inhaled deeply, trying to regain the air that was knocked out of him. "You can have my wallet," Rashaun pleaded as he opened the car door.

"Me no want your wallet. Me want to talk to you." Fish said, as he got into the car next to Rashaun.

"Drive then, and make a right at the light. If you look at me, I'm going to shoot you!" Fish said sternly, as Rashaun started the car.

"If it's the car you want, just let me off right here and you can take it."

"Shut up and drive! We got business to talk about. Me no want your money, car or clothes."

"What you want?" Rashaun nervously asked.

"Turn here."

Rashaun obeyed the commands from Fish, and drove through the streets of Brooklyn, eventually pulling up in front of a garage nearby the water.

"Get out." Fish ordered, as Rashaun turned the car off.

"What are we doing here?' Rashaun asked, totally frightened and confused.

Fish pulled the garage door open and motioned with the gun for Rashaun to get into the garage. He flipped the light on, and pulled the door back down. "Rashaun Jones, criminal lawyer, murderer."

"What the fuck are you talking about?" Rashaun asked, astounded at the statement.

"Me know you well, man. I did my research. I could ave been killed you, but me wanted to talk to you first. Sit down on the floor over there." Fish pointed to the middle of the garage that was covered with a large plastic sheet.

"Are you going to tell me what this is about?" Rashaun asked, a feeling of hopelessness coming over him.

"In due time, my boy, in due time. Now, put your hands behind your back." Fish demanded, as he pointed the muzzle of the gun in the back of Rashaun's head.

"Alright." Rashaun did as he was told, and put his hands back, so that Fish could tie them with thick white plastic zip ties.

"Now, we will start." Fish put down the gun and pulled a long knife from a bag he had placed in the corner of the room.

"What is this about?" Rashaun asked, desperately trying to loosen the ties, in order to release the tension in his arms.

"Look at me, boy. Does this face look familiar?"

"I have never met you a day in my life."

"Me know that. I want to know if I look like someone from the past." Fish said, his tone was now becoming angrier.

"Fuck, no!' Rashaun yelled, moving around to shake the cramping in his legs.

"Let me remind you. About five years ago, you killed a man."

"What?" Rashaun's memory now came back to him with a vengeance. "Are you talking about Paul?"

"Yeah, Paul was my brother."

"I'm sorry about that, but Paul was trying to kill my woman. I didn't have a choice."

"Well, I don't have a choice now, but to kill you!" Fish shouted, drawing the knife, and resting it under Rashaun's throat. "Have you ever seen them drain the blood from a pig? They cut the throat, and then they place a bucket under it, just like this one."

Fish took a black bucket and placed it on the ground, directly under Rashaun's throat. He took the knife and made a small incision, from the left of Rashaun's throat, all the way to the right. A small trail of blood now started to leak from the cut.

"I didn't have a choice.' Rashaun said, his voice now beginning to tremble. "It was either I kill him, or else he'd kill my wife."

"So, you shot him up!" Fish said, turning the knife around in his hand. "Every time I go around your throat, the cut will get deeper and deeper."

"I'm sorry for hurting your brother, but like I said, I didn't have a choice. My wife was pregnant with our first child, and your brother was going to kill them both. Do you think I would be a free man today, if I hadn't killed your brother in self defense? Look at me! I have a wife and a child, and another one on the way! I know the value of life!" Rashaun desperately pleaded with Fish for mercy.

"You nah know the value of a life, because if you did, you wouldn't have killed my brother."

"I'm sorry, I tried my best not to do it, but your brother wouldn't stop going at my woman. I would never kill a man. Life is too precious and short for that." Rashaun said, while moving around a little more, in order to relieve the pressure from his knees.

"Me and my brother were tight from small. We used to do everything together. He was the best brother in the world." Fish said, moving the sharp blade of the knife over his palm. "But now, he ain't there no more, because of you."

"You said you looked into my past, but if you had, you would know that I have never hurt a man before. Your brother's death still haunts me to this day. If I could have stopped him any other way, I would have done it. Now, I have a son and another child on the way. I know how precious life is." Rashaun moved his hands around the tie that was restricting the flow of the blood to his fingers. "I cannot tell you how sorry I was about your brother's death."

"Sorry, can't bring him back." Fish said. "He gone for good."

"I know that, and I won't even try to understand how you feel. I lost my mother a few years ago in a shooting, and up until today, I can't forget about it. She was a good woman. But, she also taught me how to move on with my life. She didn't want anger and revenge to destroy the life I had to live. I'm begging you to forgive me for what I did to your brother. I swear to God, that I didn't do it intentionally." Rashaun cried, with tears streaming from his eyes, down his face. "I want to go home to my family. I have a young son, and a girl on the way, and I want to see them grow up."

"I'm sure my brother wanted to have a family, too. But you made sure that he would never have that. Now, you beg for your life, like it was better than my brother's!" Fish brought the knife back to Rashaun's throat.

"Man, I can't tell you what to do. You are holding all the cards here. You can kill me, and I see you are well prepared to do just that. I'm not going to ask you again to spare my life. I will just ask one favor from you, and I don't care how, or when you do it."

"What's that?"

"I had a big fight with my wife yesterday, because she thought I had gone and cheated on her. I want you to tell her for me, that I never once slept with another woman. I want her to know that she was the best thing that ever happened to me, and no matter what anyone says, I didn't cheat on her. I love her, and I will see her when we reunite under the shadow of God."

"Why you wife think you fuck a gal?"

"Because the gal did a DNA test that proved that I was the father of her child."

"So how the girl get your child and you didn't fuck her?"

"I don't know.'

Rashaun shook his head. "I really wanted to prove to her that I didn't sleep with the girl, but I guess I never will get the opportunity to do it now, and that's why I want her to know that I told you that, before I died."

"That's all you want?" Fish asked.

"Yeah, she is the best thing that ever happened to me in my whole life. You ever been in love?"

"What does that mean?"

"If you know anything about life, you would know that life is worthless without love. My woman showed me that. And let me give you some advice, before you ever walk away from your woman or man."

"Bloodcloth, boy, you calling me a batty boy!"

"I'm not calling you anything, but in this day and age you, don't want to offend anyone. They got batty boys in Jamaica, too. You know that."

"True." Fish replied.

"Just always tell your woman you love her, no matter if you're going to the corner store, or to another country. This life is not promised to anyone for either a second or an hour." Rashaun said. "Now, I'm going to stop talking. Just promise me that you will tell my wife that I'm innocent."

"You finish?"

"Yeah, it's time to leave. Do what you have to do." Rashaun said, and lifted his head up, as more blood started to trickle down from his throat, and tears began to fall from his eyes.

Andria was getting restless. She hadn't heard from Rashaun in three days. He didn't pick up Wisdom up at school, and he hadn't even called to tell him goodnight. Rashaun never went to sleep, without calling to wish his son goodnight. She picked up the phone and searched for Tyrone's number. She found it, and dialed it.

"Who is this?" Tyrone asked, as he answered the phone.

"It's Andria," she said. "Have you spoken to Rashaun?"

"No, I haven't spoken to him since last week. Is everything okay?"

"Yes, if you hear from him, please ask him to call home." Andria said.

"Will do that." Tyrone replied.

Again, Andria went through the phone, until she found Lance's number. She dialed it quickly.

"Hello." Lance answered.

"Hi Lance, it's Andria. I'm looking for Rashaun. Have you seen or heard from him? The last time I saw him was about three days ago. I have been calling his cell phone constantly, but it keeps going directly into voicemail. I went by his job, but he isn't there.   "Have you spoken to his dad?" lance asked

"Yes. I called his dad, but his dad doesn't know where he is, either. I'm getting very worried. I know he has your truck, but I haven't seen that either."

"Damn, and I disabled the tracking system in the truck last week."

"Do you think I should call the police?" Andria asked.

"No, let me look around first, and if I don't find him by this evening, then you should go and file a police report," Lance said.

"Okay, I will wait for your call." Andria said, and hung up the phone.

"Where is daddy?" Wisdom asked, as he walked into the living room, with his Nintendo DSI in his hand.

Andria didn't know how to answer that question, because she honestly didn't know where Rashaun was. "I don't know, I'm waiting for him to call."

"He hasn't called in three days, and when is he coming back home? I miss my daddy," Wisdom said, climbing into Andria's lap.

"I'm sure we will hear from your Daddy soon," Andria said. "What game are you playing?"

"Mario cart."

"What's Mario cart?"

"Look, Mommy, Daddy and I play it all the time."

"Okay," Andria said, as she got up from the kitchen table. "Would you like something to eat?"

"Can I have macaroni and cheese?" Wisdom asked.

"Macaroni and cheese, coming right up."

"I hope daddy comes home soon, and maybe he could eat with me," Wisdom said, as his focus went back to his game.

Andria squeezed her eyes shut tightly. Wisdom was asking for Rashaun all the time now. She had run out of things to tell him. How much longer could she go on like this? She missed him so much, too.

Kim was surprised that she hadn't heard from Rashaun. He didn't call or come by in a rage. She was wondering if she hadn't played her cards right. She had driven by their house to see if she would see him, but he was nowhere in sight. She called his cell phone, and it went straight into voice mail. She had seen Andria and Wisdom go in and out of the house a few times, but there was no sign of Rashaun. She knew that Andria would kick him out of the house, but she still had expected to get some type of a reaction from him. There were very few women that would put up with a husband that had a child around the same time when they had theirs. She expected it to be over between Andria and Rashaun, but she had also expected Rashaun to come after her. That was where George was going to come in. George was a buffer between her and Rashaun. Eventually, she wouldn't need the buffer, and would then get rid of George. Rashaun would also want to see Raqueen, and knew that she could slowly weave him into her life. She had already made Rashaun guardian for Raqueen if anything happen to her. She had also inquired about getting a job with one of the top law firms in the city. With her father's help, she knew that the job would be waiting for her. But first, she had to work her way into the life of the man she came to New York for. Now, she had to find him. Her cell phone rang, and she picked it up, when she saw that it was George calling.

"What's up, Honey?" she spoke into the phone.

"I had the strangest call from Andria," George said.

Kim became very nervous. "What did she want?"

"She wanted to know if I had heard from Rashaun."

"She doesn't know that you and Rashaun aren't friends anymore?"

"I don't know. I asked her what was wrong, and she said nothing."

"Did she say anything else?"

"That was the strange part. She just said okay, and hung up the phone."

"You are right, that is strange." Kim released the tight grip she had on the phone.

"Oh well, maybe there is trouble in paradise?"

Kim looked at the time on the wall. "I'm hungry."

"Me, too," George answered.

"What you want to eat?"

"Besides you? I think there is this Rasta Pasta that I heard someone at work talking about today. I think I want to try it. It's at this restaurant called "Footprints," on Clarendon Road in Brooklyn. You game?"

"Yeah, why not."

"I will be over in thirty."

"See you then," Kim said, and hung up the phone.

Chapter XVIII

"*H*i Mommy, it's really beautiful up here." Rashaun said to his mom, as he floated in the air.

"Yes, it's very peaceful and quiet here." Albertina replied, watching the excitement in her son's eyes.

"Is it really over, Mommy?" Rashaun was now looking at the bright lights all around him.

"No Rashaun, you are not dead. It is not time for you yet. There are a lot of things that you need to do on earth, before you join me."

"Then, how come I am here?" Rashaun asked, now feeling a little unsure of him.

"Have you ever wondered what happens when people are knocked unconscious? Yes, they go into nothingness," Rashaun replied.

"No, my son, there is no such thing as nothingness. Human beings live in the third dimension, and that is all they know. When something traumatic happens, they go into another dimension that had always existed, but they have never experienced. It's the dimension where you converse with spirits and you see and hear things, that most people think is impossible."

"But where is my body?"

"Your body is on a street in Brooklyn, and you are about to wake up."

"I like it here."

"Yes, there isn't anything to be afraid of here. Man's biggest enemy, fear, doesn't exist in this dimension. But it also doesn't have to exist in the third dimension, either. Conquer fear and you have freed yourself, once and for all. Now, get up." With that, Albertina disappeared.

Rashaun felt a throbbing pain in the back of his head. At the same time, he felt someone nudging him on the arm. He slowly opened his eyes.

"Sir, you cannot park here!" The female traffic cop yelled, while her eyes penetrated his face, looking for abnormalities.

"Okay." Rashaun grumbled, as he looked around for the truck keys. The keys were in the ignition. He turned the key and the truck roared to life, sending a jolt of pain up his back and throughout his head. He looked around, trying to figure out where he was, but was still happy, just to be alive. He rummaged through his pocket, looking for his cell phone, but then he remembered that the car had the date and the time displayed in the dashboard. It was now 10:30, on Saturday morning. He had been knocked out for approximately three days. Immediately, he thought about Andria and Wisdom. He got out of the car and looked in the back seat, but the phone wasn't there. He didn't think Paul's brother wanted the cell phone, and thought that it had to be somewhere in the car. He popped the trunk, and discovered the phone there. He picked it up and closed the trunk. When he tried to turn the phone on, it wouldn't work. As expected, the battery was dead. He brought the phone to the front and hooked it up to the car charger. He immediately dialed Andria's cell phone.

"Rashaun? Rashaun, is it you?" Andria was excited and tearful at the same time.

"Yes, Baby it's me!" Rashaun answered.

"Come home, Baby! Come home right now! We need to see you! Forget about what happened, I just need you back here!" She pleaded, her voice now hitting peaks and valleys.

"I am. I just need to get my bearings. Did you hear from Lance?" Rashaun asked.

"Yes, he had been trying to get in touch with you since Thursday," Andria replied.

"Okay, I will be home soon, but first I have to get in touch with Lance."

"Honey, I missed you so much. And I'm so sorry for everything that has happened." Andria's voice was now strained with emotion. "I didn't know how much I would miss you, until you were gone."

"Me too, baby. I miss you guys more than I could possibly say. I will be home in a few." Rashaun said, looking at the different street signs. He had been here once before, he was sure of it.

"Bye, and hurry home!" She cried.

"I will." Rashaun hung up the phone, and immediately pulled up Lance's number.

"Rashaun?" Lance answered the phone.

"Yeah, it's me."

"What the fuck happened to you?"

"It's a long story, I will tell you later. Did you find out anything?"

"Yeah, I found out that you were right. Kim had the baby by artificial insemination." "It's all we could find out. Don't know where she got your sperm from, and we might never know. The detective said that only Kim could tell you that." Lance said.

"You need the paperwork to show your lady?"

"No, I don't think I will need it. I think she will believe me."

"Well, if you need it, I have it here, along with the lab tests and everything.'

"How the hell did he get all that?"

"In this recession, everyone is hurting. Even doctors."

"Where is Front and York Street?" Rashaun asked, looking up at the signs on the street.

"Man, that is Dumbo, and there are some nice restaurants there. It is right under the Brooklyn Bridge. I used to mess with a waitress down there. I haven't been there in a while, though. Are you planning on going there anytime soon?"

"Nothing like that, I'm headed home. I haven't seen my wife and kid in more than three days. I will give you a call tomorrow, to tell you what happened."

"Alright man, talk to you later."

Rashaun put the truck in gear, and started to drive down Front Street. He saw Jay Street, and immediately knew how to get out of the area. It wasn't long before Rashaun had hit Eastern Parkway, and headed home. He parked the car, and was greeted by Andria and Wisdom, who were both running down the driveway. He kissed Andria, and lifted Wisdom into his arms, even though he felt excruciating pain in his head.

"Are you okay?" Andria asked when she saw the expression on Rashaun's face.

"Not really, but I'm alive." Rashaun said, putting Wisdom down.

He held Andria's hand with one hand, and Wisdom with his other. When they went inside, Andria told Wisdom to go and finish the book he was reading. Andria and Rashaun went into the room. Once they got there, Rashaun went and took a shower. When he came out, Andria was sitting on the bed waiting for him.

"What happened to you?" she asked, as he dried his skin.

"Well, I ran into Paul's brother." He said, putting the towel back on the rack.

"What? Paul, my ex-boyfriend?" Andria asked, looking lost.

"Yes, that Paul."

"All of Paul's family lives in Jamaica."

"Well, his brother came up to settle the score."

"Oh no, Rashaun, I'm so sorry," Andria said, running to Rashaun.

Rashaun hugged her. "What are you sorry for, you didn't do anything wrong."

"It's my entire fault. I brought this into your life."

"Let's not talk about bringing the past into each other's life, because I think I'm far guiltier of that, than you." Rashaun said, sitting down on the bed.

"Paul mentioned his brother a few times. I think his name was Banjo but he always called him Fish.."

"Well, let's just say we didn't exchange names. He was more interested in seeing me take a dirt nap."

"So, what happened?"

"Well Fish, now that I know his name, picked me up from work and forced me to go with him, by putting a gun in my ribs." Rashaun said.

"Oh, my God!" Andria muttered.

"He took me to a garage in Dumbo, you know, the place under the bridge."

"Yeah, I have heard of it, even though I have never been there. Go on."

"When we got there, he tied me up and brought a knife to my throat, then proceeded to tell me why he was going to slit me. Well, I pleaded for my life, hoping I would be able to see my family again. When I thought that it wasn't working, I made preparations to meet my maker."

"Are you serious?" Andria sounded amazed.

I woke up with a nasty headache in the truck on a street in Dumbo." Rashaun got up from the bed, as naked as the day he was born. He went into the dresser drawer, and pulled out a black pair of boxer shorts.

"He must have knocked you out. That would account for the big bump on the back of your head. I wonder what you said to him that made him spare your life."

Rashaun pulled up his jeans. "Well, I'm not concerned about that, I'm just happy that I'm alive."

"Do you think he will try to get you again?" Andria asked, with a measure of concern still in her voice.

"No, I think he got the answer he came here for." Rashaun said, as he slipped a T-shirt over his head.

"Where are you going?" Andria asked.

"I also found out that Kim got pregnant by artificial insemination."

"What! That bitch." Andria got up off of the bed.

"I'm going to have a conversation with her. I want to know where she got my sperm," Rashaun said.

"Honey, I'm so sorry I doubted you, when you told me that you hadn't been unfaithful."

"Well, I could understand why, with this overwhelming evidence facing you."

"But still, it was my fault. I should have gone with my feelings. I let reasoning overcome the feelings in my heart, and I'm sorry for that."

"Well, it's over now. I just need to have a talk with Kim, so that this never happens again." Rashaun said.

"Not this time, Rashaun."

"What do you mean?"

"Kim didn't come to you. This time she came to me. I will have a talk with Kim."

"Honey, I don't think that's a good idea."

"Trust me Rashaun, it's the only way. Kim has fucked with us for the last time."

"What! Andria, you cursed!"

"Yeah, so you know how I feel. And you should know that it's futile to try to stop me."

Rashaun looked at the fire that was now in his wife's eyes. "I don't want this thing getting any worse than it already is."

"Trust me, it won't. If Kim wants a fight, then she will have a fight."

Rashaun walked over to Andria. "Now I'm very worried, because you are pregnant."

"Don't worry about that. This baby has received enough stress to last a lifetime. I won't let Kim create any more, and I have to do this." Andria said, holding on to Rashaun. "I promise you that everything will be alright."

"I will have a woman to woman talk with her."

Rashaun looked at his wife. He heard what she was saying, but somehow, he felt that Andria and Kim would do a lot more than talk. He knew that he had to get to Kim before his wife did.

"Okay Baby, but be careful."

Kim received the long awaited call from Andria, and gave her the address of her apartment building. She tried to change the time until later, but Andria seemed agitated, and wouldn't hear of it. This was bad timing, because George was also on his way over. He had told her that his phone was dying, and that he had left his car charger at home. Kim still kept on trying to reach him, because she didn't want him interrupting Andria's visit. She didn't know what would transpire between them. What she did know was that Andria and Rashaun's relationship was over. It was doomed in the doctor's office, when she saw the look on Andria's face. It was a look devoid of love, for the person that caused her that pain. It was that look of betrayal that so many women and men have experienced. She could tell that Rashaun had become part of Andria's world, and now, he had taken that world from her. Yes, it was the same look Rashaun had so many years ago, when he found out about her and Derek. It was a look that to this day, she regretted causing, but that was now in the past. Atonement was finally within her reach. Kim was feeling really good about this meeting. With Andria out of the way, she knew that she still couldn't just walk back into Rashaun's life. No, it was going to take time. He would need to spend some time with his daughter, Raqueen. Yes, Rashaun would definitely want to spend time with Raqueen. She also expected him to question her about how Raqueen was conceived, but that was a secret that she would take to her grave. After accepting the fact that she would never tell him, his love for his daughter would then be complete. Eventually, he would realize that he also wanted to spend some time with her, and the feelings that he had buried so long ago for her, would now start rising to the surface. She would give him anything he wanted. She would do anything that he wanted her to do. There would be a big transition in their lives. History had shown that hatred could turn into love, and that's exactly what was going to happen with them. Yes, she came to New York to get her man, and she was going to do just that.

Andria heard about people renting apartments and paying more than three thousand dollars a month for only a one bedroom place. She was certain that this was one of those expensive apartment buildings. The door-man let her in, and told her that she could go right up, because Kim was expecting her. She thanked him, and headed towards the elevator that would take her to the ninth floor. The building itself smelled like fresh apricots, and beautiful plants were located in strategic points in the hallway. The elevator barely made a sound, as it took her up to the ninth floor. She barely had a chance to touch the bell, when Kim suddenly appeared, and opened the door. She walked in with a sense of purpose.

If truth be told, Andria didn't know exactly what she was going to say to Kim. She knew that what she really wanted to do was to grab Kim by the neck and squeeze it, until she stopped breathing. She wanted to punch her in the face, until her face became like Jell-O, with holes in it. She hated the woman that was now showing her to the couch, wearing a look of confidence on her face. Andria smiled inwardly, because she knew that Kim thought she had accomplished her goal. She looked like a squirrel holding a nut, or an Olympian, wearing the gold medal, or even Obama winning the presidency. Yes, Kim smirked, it was a great feat accomplished.

"Can I get you something to drink?" Kim asked, her voice betraying the euphoria she was now feeling.

"No, because this won't take long," Andria replied, and refused to take a seat on Kim's couch.

"Suit yourself." Kim responded, becoming a little agitated.

"When exactly did you sleep with my husband for him to impregnate you?" Andria asked, her voice sounding soft and controlled.

"What! Why is that important?" Kim's tone was a bit nasty.

"I wanted to know if you guys fucked or made love, because there is a difference, you know."

"I can't believe this."

"You can't believe what, Kim? You said that my husband impregnated you, and I just wanted to know under what circumstances. Did you suck his dick, too?"

"My, my, Rashaun's little saint, has a dirty little mouth."

"No Kim, just because I don't speak or act like a whore, that doesn't mean that I don't know how to behave like one. It's just that I prefer to do it under the sheets, if you know what I mean, and with my husband."

"Obviously, you haven't been doing that good of a job, because he was all up in mine." Kim said, wondering what the fuck was going on, and feeling now that this woman was playing with her.

Andria continued. "I know my husband, and while I can't swear for anyone, I know that my man was never with you."

"So, how do you explain our child?" Kim asked, feeling a tremendous burden overcome her.

"On a beautiful night, my husband and I got together and decided to bring another being into this world. We didn't get it right the first time, so do you want me to tell you how many more times we did, it until I became pregnant? Or, should I show you the video? Oh, I'm sorry you have your own video. What was his name, Derek?"

"I think you should leave now!" Kim's face now looked contorted.

"Why Kim, where is your test tube baby?" Andria said.

"What!" a look of total surprise froze Kim's face.

"Yes Kim, I know that my husband's dick never touched you at all. A test tube did, and your child was conceived from plastic."

Kim started to cry.

Andria looked at her and actually felt pity for her.

"Rashaun loves me! He always will! I hate you!" The tears came down in torrents now, as her body started shaking.

"It's over Kim, and now you can go back to the hole where you came from." Andria said and turned around to leave.

At the same time, George opened the door to the apartment. Andria gave him a look of disgust as he entered.

"I love him!" Kim shouted, "He will always be mine!"

Andria looked over at George whose eyes were now wide open in disbelief. "Andria!"

Andria turned around, but it was too late.

George didn't have a choice. The woman that he loved wasn't stopping. The knife she held was raised high, and she was moving too quickly for him to stop her.

"Rashaun will always be mine!" Kim screamed, as the knife came down from the top of her head.

George pushed Andria down on the floor, and stepped directly in the path of the knife, trying to protect her. The knife sank deep into his chest, piercing his spine. George crumbled to the floor, with the knife still in his chest, and with Kim still holding onto the handle.

Andria screamed as she saw the blood gush from George's chest. A white middle aged woman was walking by with her poodle, when she heard all the screaming, she ran into the apartment.

"What happened?" she yelled, and immediately pressed 911 on her cell phone.

Chapter XIX

*T*he boat was anchored a few miles from the shore. The woman was constantly looking overboard. She held a hook in her hand. A netted trap bubbled to the surface of the water next to the boat, and she quickly hooked it.

"You can let it go now, I've got it," she said, and immediately felt the full weight of the trap. She looked to the back of the boat and a saw a long dark figure climb aboard. He was removing his swimming glasses, as he entered the boat.

"You are getting the hang of this," Fish said to his wife, Mindi.

"Yeah, it's good being out here with you." Mindi said, as she stepped back from the side of the boat, giving Fish enough room so that he could haul in the trap.

"Yeah, me miss this bad." Fish said, as he removed the fish from the trap.

"We are having crab tonight!" Mindi exclaimed, delighted to find a two foot long crab in the trap. "I'm going to curry down its tail."

"Do you know that they sell imitation crab in the States?"

"No! Who would eat imitation crab?"

"A lot of people do. Some even feel that it tastes even better than real crab."

"What do they make it with?"

"I think it's plastic. They make everything with plastic in the States."

Fish dropped the trap back into the water. "We have one more hour to go."

"Me tired," Mindi said and sat back down in the boat.

"You want to rest out here for a little while?" Fish asked, looking over at Mindi, who was dressed in form fitting shorts and a tight wife beater shirt.

"Rest was not what I had in mind," Mindi whispered, as she pulled her top over her head. "It's a beautiful sunny day and I'm so hot."

"You need some water to cool you down." Fish then dipped a bucket into the sea.

"You nah wet me." Mindi warned, pointing her finger at Fish.

Fish threw the bucket of water at Mindi, soaking her good. "I'm going to kill you!"

In a few seconds, Fish was holding Mindi's hand, as she found her own bucket. He held her hands and took the bucket, dipping it into the sea once again. "Now, what did you say?"

"Fish, I swear, if you do that…"

Fish emptied the bucket over Mindi's head. Then, he threw it towards the front of the boat. At the same time, his lips found hers and they sank down in the boat, kissing each other passionately.

They were now lying naked in the middle of the boat. Looking up at the sky, they saw the plane with the DELTA name printed on it, flying above them.

"The Americans are coming." Fish said. "Come back to Jamaica, man."

"Do you miss the U.S.?" Mindi asked.

"Not really, but there are some good people over there." Fish said, and for a moment, his eyes became cloudy.

"But they eat plastic crabs."

"Yeah." He said. "They are crazy."

"Some of them are."

"You're not going back there, are you?"

"No Baby, I have what I want right here." He whispered, and began kissing her neck.

"Are you sure?" Mindi asked. "You didn't tell me what happened in the U.S."

"This is Jamaica honey, and what happened in the U.S., stays in the U.S."

"Yeah that's what mi say, too. What happened in Jamaica, stays in Jamaica."

Fish paused for a second and looked down at his wife, as she pulled him close to her, wearing a big smile.

"Are you going to give it to me, or not?" Mindi said, while she gazed up at the Jamaican airplane that was heading for the States. She was definitely sure that he would come back to Jamaica.

◎◎◎

"Where is he?" Rashaun asked.

"He is out in the backyard." Valarie said.

Rashaun opened the back door and walked outside.

"I see you found time for an old friend." George said, as he turned around.

"Yeah, I came here to see what a bull shitter is up to." Rashaun replied, continuing his stride towards George.

"Can't be up to anything lately." George said, "I'm back in the pen."

"Your wife is a good woman, and she took you back, even after all that went on." Rashaun took a seat next to George.

"I know. I'm blessed, whether I deserve it or not." George sighed, slowly turning around. "I just have to get used to it."

"Yeah, so do I."

"But, we can still go out and have a beer, right?" George asked.

"George, I owe you a lot more than a beer."

"I did the only thing a man could do. You owe me nothing. How is she, anyway?" George asked.

"I don't know. I'm going there today."

"Are you taking Raqueen?"

"Yeah, I don't have a choice, since she lives with me now. Besides, that's her mother."

"How is she adjusting to living with you?"

"I think she is doing fine. She and Wisdom get along great."

"And what about Andria?"

"Well, you know that Andria's heart is as big as the ocean."

"When is the baby due?"

"This is the last month of her pregnancy."

"Congratulations, man."

"Yeah, thanks."

"What keys do you have in your hand there?"

Rashaun turned the keys over in his hand. "Lance gave me the X6."

George just shook his head. "Damn, that guy is living large. I would love to be in his place, with all that money and pussy."

Rashaun laughed. "I don't know which one is worse."

"Tell me about it. Stand back a second, I'm still learning how to use this thing." George maneuvered the wheelchair around. "They got all these different gears on these things. They told me it has a top speed of 10 miles per hour. Like, I'm planning on racing with it."

"Maybe you should read the manual?"

George looked at Rashaun. "I'm still a man, you know. I just have to strengthen the tongue."

"George, you will never change."

"Thanks." George reached out to knuckle with Rashaun.

"I brought you some of that tea that you like to drink."

"Thanks, man. I heard people say that if you drink this tea, it will make your dick rise. That's why I drink it every day, and I'm hoping that maybe a miracle is on its way."

"Are you having that operation next week?"

"Yeah, there is this new stem cell shit they're doing. I don't care, and I told them that they could experiment with my ass, because I want to be able to fuck again."

Rashaun felt a lump form in his throat. "I will be there for you."

"Thanks, bro."

Rashaun started the car.

"How is he doing?" Andria asked.

"He is all right." Rashaun said, looking back and pulling out from the curb. He looked over at her.

"I know, Rashaun, I have to go and see him." Andria said.

"Yes, you do." Rashaun replied. "He doesn't blame you for what happened."

"I don't care if he blames me. I blame myself. Your friend took a knife for me, and in the process, he became crippled for life." Andria's voice was heavy, as she looked back at George's house.

"I understand that, but I think you need to go see him yourself, and thank him for saving your life. I think that will help him recover a little."

"Rashaun, how could I do that? How could I face his wife and his child?" Andria's voice was now becoming tense.

Rashaun heard the stress in her voice, and tried to reassure her. "Okay, I'm sure you will go when you are ready. Are you okay with going over there?"

"Yeah, I'm okay with it. Look at the children, playing with their games. It's like they are in a world of their own."

"That's a good thing, because the way things are going, their adult-hood won't be a walk in the park." Rashaun went from focusing on Wisdom and Raqueen who were both sitting in the backseat, to the road ahead.

"How long are they going to keep her?" Andria asked. "Because I feel sometimes that this is too convenient for her. It's as though she planned the whole thing."

Rashaun kept his eyes on the road. "I know she is devious, but I don't think that this was the ending she had in mind."

Andria looked out the window. "You never know."

◎◎◎

"We will stay outside just in case something happens," Said the big burly guard, as Rashaun opened the door. He let Raqueen go in first then, he followed right behind her.

"Hi, Mom," Raqueen said, and went over and kissed Kim on the cheek. She hugged her mother and played with her hands.

Kim just stared at the walls.

Rashaun stood by the door, looking at Kim.

She had on a blue hospital dress and her wrist was bandaged. She didn't look at him or at her daughter. Instead, her eyes continued to pierce the wall.

Raqueen continued to talk to her mother, even though she didn't respond. She told her about her new bedroom and all about Wisdom and her friends at the new school. She also told her mother about the great grades she received on her tests, and how smart her teacher said she was.

Rashaun continued to look at Kim, who continued to sit there, void of any emotion.

After a few minutes, Rashaun told Raqueen that it was time to leave, and he reached for her hand. "Your mom is not feeling well today, but maybe she will be better the next time you visit."

"What's wrong with her?" Raqueen sadly asked.

"I don't know, and as I told you earlier, the doctor is running some more tests on her soon and maybe they will be able to treat her, once they get the results.

"Okay. Mommy, I'll see you next week." Raqueen said.

Rashaun looked at Kim one last time and walked out the door. He returned his pass to the front desk and continued walking out of the building.

"Are you okay?" Rashaun asked Raqueen holding onto her hand.

"No, I don't like coming to this place. Why can't we bring Mommy home? Andria could take care of her." She said, searching Rashaun's face for understanding.

"No, we can't do that. Your mom is not well, and she needs special treatment, and this is the only place she can receive the treatment."

"Well why can't she even go outside? Why does she have to stay behind all of those locked doors?" she asked.

"Well, that's the way they designed this place, and it is the best place for her to be right now." Rashaun explained.

"Well, I don't like it, and as soon as I get big enough, I'm taking my

Mommy out of there." Raqueen said.

Rashaun got into the car.

"How is she?" Andria asked.

"The same." Rashaun replied.

"I don't trust that woman, money and evilness is a bad combination. You know she won't stop until she gets what she wants or the ultimate price is paid." Andria said looking out the window.

"Babes, Kim is history. Look at the kids in the back, fast asleep without a care in the world." Rashaun said looking over his shoulders.

"Let's hope it stays like that." Andria said wishing it more than believing it.

◎◎◎

After they left, Kim got up and walked over to the window. She looked out and saw Rashaun and Raqueen walking together towards the car. Andria and Wisdom were waiting outside for them. When they saw Rashaun and Raqueen approaching, they all went back into the car together. A faint smile appeared on Kim's lips as she watched them drive away.

"It's not over." She whispered, directing her comment to the quickly disappearing SUV.

OTHER NOVELS BY

MICHAEL PRESLEY

TEARS ON A SUNDAY AFTERNOON

Chapter 1

Twenty years later

I was pushed through the revolving exit door of the office building by two ladies rushing to leave. They stared at me as if I had interrupted their flight into the streets. I smiled knowing that I could make them walk right back into the building and forget about the kids and the husbands at home. Another day, I would have done just that, but today I already had plans. As I walked through the corridor leading to the elevators, I was constantly bumped by hoards of people heading to the revolving doors. I looked at my gold Movado watch and saw that it was ten after five. I navigated to the line of elevators that carried the workers up and down every day. I stepped aside as more than a dozen business people in suits pushed themselves off one of the elevators. I had been in the building earlier to set up a project with a group of engineers from our office. It was an extensive project that would require long, tedious hours. It was similar to one we had done on Staten Island a few weeks ago. During that visit, I met one of the secretaries, Donna Smith, who had been with the company for five years. One of my coworkers, Brian, a tall dark fellow from Brooklyn, introduced me. The first hour we were in the building, Brian had spent at least forty-five minutes trying to talk to Donna. I paid very little attention to the both of them because unlike me, Brian was single and the world was his oyster. I have to take a different path with women, a path that denotes understanding. Marriage somewhat limits the playing field. I always tell the women that I'm interested in that I'm married and to tell you the truth it hasn't made a damn difference in whether we fuck or not. My pretty face is all that I need.

Brian and I had ate lunch almost everyday since I came onboard at Reason Consulting, the largest black engineering firm in New York. Engineers at Reason were not hired based on their résumés, but from recommendations by one of the company's board members. My father-in-law had me working there a few months after the wedding. During our lunch at Au Bon Pan, Brian told me that Donna was dripping for me.

TEARS ON A SUNDAY AFTERNOON

I looked at him as if he was crazy. I hadn't said a word to the woman and she was "dripping for me." This was not extraordinary for me because I have had women that have taken off their panties the first time I walked into their apartments. It's the life of a pretty boy.

Brian is a cool guy; he doesn't have a jealous bone in his body. He told me that he tried talking to her but she was only interested in me. So after speaking to Brian, I went over to her. When I got to her desk, she stood and shook my hand. I must tell you I was very impressed. She was about five feet nine inches tall, dark complexion with a body that almost any man would crawl after. I said almost any man, not me. I have had those women whom men have killed themselves over. During our conversation, she told me to hold on because she had to file an important document. When she turned around, I'll just say that she was a black man's butter: all a man wanted to do was spread it.

I showed the security guard my temporary ID that I had received to gain easy access into the building. I had left the building at 2:00 P.M. to go and pick up my son, Emerald, from school. I didn't have to do that, but when I got a break at work, I tried to spend as much time with him as possible. My grandmother and my son are my only true loves. I stepped into the empty elevator and pressed the button for the twenty- fifth floor.

It was approximately five-fifteen when I knocked on the office door. She opened the door, led me to a couch in front of her desk and told me to wait. A few minutes passed and a man I hadn't seen before came out and spoke to her briefly as he walked out of the office. He had a large Kenneth Cole briefcase in his right hand and upon further inspection, I noticed a gold handcuff kept the briefcase in place.

"I'm so wound up," she said as she slumped down in her chair.

"That's work⁻ five days a week, then two days to think about it, then five days back at work," I replied.

"You're very beautiful," she said, sitting on the edge of the chair.

I have heard that comment from the time I was old enough to remember it. It had gotten me into and out of trouble. I think sometimes I could get away with murder because of my looks, the result of a crime perpetuated on my mother when she was incarcerated at the Delvin Correctional Facility in upstate New York. Three white correction officers raped her. After I was born, my mother took her life.

"I know," I said, smiling. "Thanks for the compliment."

"You're mixed aren't you?" she asked. "With that curly hair and those blue eyes, you've got to be."

"Yeah, my father is white and my mother is a southern girl."

"So, who did you inherit that six-foot slender frame from, your mother or father?"

"I don't know." I was being honest because I was never told who my father was. I guess nobody wanted to set up DNA tests for three white men.

She stood and walked to the front of the desk. "Come over here. Let me see how much taller you are than me."

It was a bullshit line, but the games had begun and the only reason I was here was because I was willing to play them.

I stood in front of her, her hard nipples pushing against my shirt. She smelled like fresh-picked apricots.

She looked up at me, her luscious red lips glistening against the dark pigmentation of her face.

"I..."

It was all she got out of her mouth as my lips joined hers. She should have slapped me then. Maybe I should have slapped myself for making such assumptions but neither of us did. Instead, her mouth feasted on mine as my hand went to the front of her blouse. The snaps came apart like dry- rotted steel wool, the kind my grandmother used to give me to scrub the burnt pots. I pulled her blouse off her shoulders and it fell onto her desk. She pulled me towards her, her breasts rubbing against my white Guess T-shirt. Her hand traveled down my chest toward my dick and she started to rub it through my pants.

"I knew you were packing, looks and a big dick. What more can a girl ask for?" she said as I helped her pull my T-shirt over my head. She started to make her way down my chest, leaving a trail of red lip marks. She unbuckled my pants and slid them down. She gently brushed the outsides of my legs with her fingertips as she reached up to pull off my Calvin Klein boxers. I stepped to the side as she gathered my clothes and put them on the couch. I stood naked on the twenty-fifth floor in an office building in the heart of Manhattan.

KEISHA'S CHOICE

Chapter 1

"Mommy did you take any of my clothes to the cleaners? It's raining and I can't find anything to wear?" Keisha Graves paced back and forth in front a closet that was about ten feet wide and four feet deep. Suddenly, her eyes connected to a pink and white outfit. She leaped into the closet almost tripping over a series of sneakers and shoes lining the floor of the closet. She pulls the outfit out and walks to the full length mirror at the right of the closet. She rests the outfit against her chest and looks into the mirror. Her face set in a contortion of unhappiness. She glanced over at the clock it showed 8:00 A. M. She stamps away from the mirror and throws the outfit back into the closet.

"Keisha, it's after 8:00 you will be late for school." Her mother, Tricia Lewis's, voice came from the room adjoining Keisha's.

"Mom, I can't find anything to wear." Keisha retorted.

"Young girl you are not serious. Your closet is full of clothes."

"But mommy it's raining I cannot wear just anything when its raining."

Keisha could hear her mother's door closed followed by her footsteps coming down the hall. There was a soft knock on Keisha's bedroom door.

"Come in mom." Keisha called not getting up from her bed.

Ms. Lewis was dressed in a light gray business suit. She had recently celebrated her thirty seventh birthday at a party in a small restaurant/bar in Brooklyn heights. She was a very attractive woman who recently started dating an accountant from the prominent accounting firm of Fen and Foster.

"Why are you still not dressed for school?" she sat down next to her daughter on the bed.

"I just can't seem to find anything to wear." Keisha responded.

Keisha's mother smiled. "You have a closet full of clothes and shoes and you can't find anything to wear."

"Mom you don't understand I can't go to school in anything. My hair was done over the weekend. I have to get something to go along with my new hair style and I have to wear something appropriate for the weather." Keisha followed her mom who had gotten up of the bed and went to Keisha's closet.

"What about this?" Ms. Lewis asked holding out an outfit for Keisha to look at.

"Too dark to wear on a rainy day."

Keisha's mother took another outfit out of the closet.

"It doesn't go with my hair."

Again Ms. Lewis mother went into the closet and pulled out another outfit.

"Definitely not!" Keisha said shaking her head.

Ms. Lewis put the outfit back and stepped away from the closet. She walked quickly to the door. "I have to be at work by 9:30. I don't have time for this."

"What I'm I suppose to do mom?" Keisha asked walking behind her mom to the door.

"Keisha, my dad and I have bought you all the clothes you asked for and you still cannot find anything to wear. You do this every morning and because of that you are late every morning. I'm not a magician, every outfit in the store cannot be at your finger tips. Even though your dad is not here he has been very supportive but you know if he sees your report card he will stop giving you an allowance. You cannot miss school for silly reasons and expect to do well."

Keisha rolled her eyes at her mom, "Here comes the lecture."

"I see you are not listening. Just get to school on time. I will see you this evening." Ms. Lewis pulled the door shut behind her.

"She doesn't understand." Keisha said as she went back into her room.

She inhaled deeply as she walked back to her closet. Her cell phone began to ring as she once more started to sift through her clothes.

"Yeah Nicole, I'm still home." Keisha said concentrating on her clothes. "Yes I know that we have a test in Mr. Klein class this morning. I will just have to miss it."

Keisha pulled an outfit from out of the closet.

"I don't care I'm failing math anyway. Mr. Klein doesn't like me and I feel the same way about him."